A Switch in Time

By

John Paul Bernett

A Switch in Time

© Copyright Author John Paul Bernett
All rights reserved. No part of this book may be reproduced, stored, or transmitted by any means—whether auditory, graphic, mechanical, or electronic—without written permission of both publisher and author, except in the case of brief excerpts used in critical articles and reviews. Unauthorized reproduction of any part of this work is illegal and is punishable by law.
ISBN: 978-0-9926173-8-7
Cover design   V-Edition Media

Printed by Book Printing UK
Remus House, Coltsfoot Drive, Peterborough, PE2 9BF

John Paul Bernett

Forward

Can the time we live in be changed by the past? Does the time we live in make us who we are? In the twilight between sleep and awake in that grey area that is a mystery to all, who or what listens to your inner most thoughts?

BE CAREFUL WHAT YOU WISH FOR, BECAUSE IT JUST MIGHT HAPPEN.

John Paul Bernett

Chapter 1

As one hour slowly drifted into another, Alicia Winters' mind still could not allow her the sleep she so desperately wanted. She was going over in fine detail the events of the previous week - the week that had started so ordinary - ordinary by her standards at least, had left her unsure as to what to do next. Indeed, would anything for her family ever be the same again? As she finally drifted into slumber, her dreams took her back as she relived the past seven days.

Monday morning began with a trip into town to view a luxury apartment on the new waterside development, situated in the old industrial part of Leeds by the river. It was an area that had been left direlect for years…and all the warehouses and factories along the waterside had grown dishevelled. Within a few short years, however, the developers had made the area into the 'place to be' – for the right price, that is.

Alicia called in at Beacroft & Dunne, the estate agents that were advertising this wonderful one-bedroom penthouse with a balcony on the river itself. 'A much sought-after apartment in the 'place to be seen in" the estate agent had said. 'It's just a short walk through the church yard', he had continued. It was winter, but the cold was no bother to Alicia; her new sheepskin-lined boots she had just paid £1,450 for were keeping her feet toasty warm. Her fur coat, a present from daddy for…well…no reason at all, really…was not only warm, but was this season's must-have fur coat. The only downside was the dread of actually *walking the whole five hundred yards through a horrible churchyard with all those unwashed, diseased, nasty dead people buried from God knows how many centuries before.*

1

A Switch in Time

Ian Steele was the unfortunate estate agent who had drawn the short straw on that particular morning, so he was the one to show her her new dwelling. This was the *twelfth* apartment she had viewed within the previous two weeks, and this was the *fourth* time Ian Steele was burdened with the task of showing her around.

"The Parish Church is a beautiful building with such pleasant surroundings...and you will be able to see it through your rear windows. I hear the bell ringers have won awards..." announced Ian with a warming smile.

"It's *hideous*...graves everywhere...and those *horrible bells*! I hope they turn them off at night, or I will be round to put a stop to them!" was Alicia's quick retort.

"Umm...sorry Miss Winters...err if you just go through the gate at the bottom there, you will see the entrance to the building...that is where the penthouse elevator is located." Said Ian with a less-confident voice.

The Penthouse apartment was *magnificent*, and would be the envy of all her friends. All, that is, except *Melissa Heatherington*, who was a complete BITCH because her daddy gave her even more money than Alicia gets! The bedroom was thirty feet square, with an enormous king-sized bed in the middle, and everything a girl could possibly want to hand. The kitchen had every modern appliance and convenience that the woman who would cook and clean for her would possibly need. The living room had full wall-length and height windows with a view only bettered by the balcony. Being a penthouse it stretched the length of the building and was *breathtaking*. Yes – this apartment befitted her lifestyle, as second-in-command at her daddy's multi-million pound haulage company. Albeit she had never worked a day there in her pampered life...but that was not a care to her, as tomorrow was her *birthday*, and looking around at her £800,000 present she thought to herself 'this will do for a while...'

John Paul Bernett

"Okay my little man…run along and get this place cleaned, I'm having a party here tomorrow."

"But Miss Winters – we have the paperwork to do, and credit checks – we couldn't possibly…"

"Let me stop you there you *little upstart*. I *want it, so that means I will HAVE IT*…so go and see to it, you CRETIN!"

"I'm *really* sorry, but I don't have the authority to…"

Once again she cut him off by putting her phone to her ear and bursting into tears. "Daddy! Deal with this!"

She threw the phone at Ian Steele and stormed into the bedroom.

Two minutes later there was a tap on the bedroom door. Nervously Ian Steele said, "It's all sorted Miss…you can move straight in today."

Alicia opened the door, looked straight at him and said, "Why are you still here? I have things to do, now GO AWAY!!"

At that point, he left the penthouse and made his way back to the estate agents. Upon arriving back at the office, he slammed his briefcase onto his desk and screamed out, "I *hate* that *spoilt bitch!*"

Graham Dunne, one of the firms partners looked at him and said, "I know how you feel, but its worse than you think…"

"How so?" Ian asked.

"I have a check for £800,000, and I can cash it…as long as I release *you* for…*insubordination*…" said Graham.

"Whoa…are you *serious*?" replied Ian.

"I'm afraid it's this check, or *you*…which means you are out. It's time to clear your desk – I'm sorry – that is just the way it is." Was his answer.

3

A Switch in Time

Alicia picked up her phone and dialled her daddy. "I approve of my little present, daddy...but I'm obviously going to need a new car. I can't park my *old thing* here...it's almost a year old, for God's sake! Can I leave that in your hands, darling? And can you have my things sent round? Bye for now..." she said with a knowing smile, tossing her phone onto the French polished table.

Alicia's father slammed his phone down in disgust. "She is sooo spoilt...nothing is EVER good enough!" growled Alfred Winters. "She needs bringing down a peg or two!" he continued.

"As if you would EVER do THAT to your little princess!" scoffed his wife Amanda.

"If my great-grandfather could see how the family haulage business had grown...and more to the point, what rich children are like in the twenty-first century, he wouldn't believe his EYES!" said Alfred.

"Ohhhh...stop going ON and ON and ONNN about your *stupid ancestors*...I'm having lunch with Monica if you need me. I will be having some retail therapy at Harvey Nichols."

With that, she picked up her wallet of credit cards, placed them in her Gucci handbag, and left.

*Bye, dear...*thought Alfred, as the realization that his whole family were *completely and utterly SPOILT ROTTEN*. All, that is, except his only son Jamie...James Albert Winters...who was not spoilt at all. The only money he had ever asked for from his father was a small loan to start his own business. To his father's dismay, Jamie had shunned the easy life of the family business; he had backpacked his way around the world when he left university, to see what the real world was like. He wanted to be an engineer. He had a passion for history, and it was his favourite subject at school, and to Jamie the Industrial Revolution was the single-most important part. In fact, he had based his business upon that very era. In truth, his business was an extension of his hobby. He was not in it for the money – he didn't really have need of money. His was NOT the life of the Armani-suited, upwardly-mobile jet-set. His life was dirty hands, overalls, and a cheese sandwich at the pub with his only work stuff and backpacking buddy Freddy Chambers. He procured a start-up grant from his father to buy four miles of old railway track, a broken down old steam engine, a third-class coach and a worn-out station complete with work shed. A pile of old rubbish to most people – but to Jamie, it was heaven on Earth, and today was TUESDAY – so it was back to work on what was going to be the world's BEST privately-preserved railway…but at the moment it was some broken track, bits and bobs of an old steam engine and what was left of a third-class coach. In his mind, he really felt he was at the start of his very own Industrial Revolution.

As ever, as the start of every working day, he wondered what joys lay ahead…oh YES! The day's only down part was it was his stupid sister's birthday party tonight. Amanda had told him to make an effort to 'be nice' as there would be many of her 'influential' friends there and she didn't want him turning up like 'that *nasty little Chambers person that you waste SO MUCH of your time with on that silly train-set thingie…*' As ever, he totally ignored her. He couldn't even call her 'mother'. Her lifestyle made him SICK TO HIS STOMACH! At least his dad had worked hard all his life to actually *earn* his money…Jamie's grandfather had made his father work up through the ranks, and he received a working insight into every aspect of haulage before he took over the family business. Even after he was Chairman of the company, he would still roll his sleeves up and fix or drive a truck if need be. Jamie looked up to his father and was very proud of his achievements.

Amanda and Monica sipped their tea in the restaurant of Harvey Nichols. They were complaining about the amount of 'common people' who had been in their favourite store.

"They *really* don't know their place!" moaned Amanda.

Monica agreed.

A Switch in Time

Amanda continued, "I wonder what it's like to be a poor retch, living in a little house, with no *real use* to society...they should be kept out of sight, and only be let out on certain days...then we wouldn't have to *look at them*!" Monica again of course agreed.

Alfred Winters sat in his favourite chair, in his own room, where no member of the family apart from Jamie ever entered. It was just a room with photos on the wall, portraying the family business down the last couple of centuries, and books about haulage in general. It was whilst he was sitting there, he wondered where he had gone wrong – and most of his family didn't respect him. In fact, they only saw him as their *personal bank*! At times like these, when Alfred felt down and alone, he would talk with his long-dead father – as we all do from time to time.

"How could I have let this happen, dad? Sometimes I don't even *recognize* my own wife and daughter! They are spoilt so much! How can I bring them down to size?"

As far as his father was concerned, his plea fell on deaf ears, but in life...sometimes when you ask a question and the person you are questioning isn't listening...someone *else* answers. Alfred fell into a deep sleep.

CHAPTER TWO

John Watson was the second child of Albert and Doris Watson. His was a simple existence; being the oldest boy, it would be him that would take over the family business, because his elder sibling was his sister – and *women* obviously *cannot* run businesses. Their roles were cooking, cleaning and steering the canal boats.

The family business was transporting coal, and the small back helmsman's cabin had been birthplace, playground, school and home for all of his 17 years. Boyhood had ended when he was six, and working began at 5 am every morning feeding and harnessing the horse Toby to the canal barge. It would end some 16 hours later. It was a hard life, but it was better than most – and in his world, he was happy with his lot in life.

Doris Watson was always first out of the bunk, and she lit the fire after collecting some kindling. It was icy that morning, and the holes in her boots let in the cold and damp, but she HAD boots and her feet would warm soon. It wasn't long before the kettle was boiling and toast was ready, so she woke her daughter Alice from her slumber to help her. When the breakfast table was laid out, Alice woke her father Albert and her brothers John and James so they could eat their breakfasts. As soon as the Watson men had eaten their breakfasts of tea and toast, they started work. Albert and John began breaking the ice that was freezing their boat to its mooring, and with long poles began cracking the ice on its starboard side. Meanwhile young James tended Toby for his long day ahead.

It was still two hours before sunrise, and what little warmth the winter sun would bring would be a welcome relief. This however

A Switch in Time

was not the time to think about warmth, it was time to think about getting to the coal bunker before everyone else, and to load up with the most powerful fuel *of all time* – COAL.

John had heard men talking about steam engines that could *run on rails*...Albert, however, convinced him that his future was safe, because nothing could *ever compete* with a horse as strong as Toby! John was not totally convinced about this...but he did say 'that's true, Dad', to make Albert feel better. On both sides of Albert's canal boat was a sign he was proud of – ALBERT WATSON & SON – showing bold and black upon what used to be bright red boards, but constant wiping off had dulled the red somewhat. At the pickup point, a long line of horse-drawn coal carts were emptying their precious cargo onto the few barges that had broken free from the morning ice. Albert's boat was third in line, so there was time for a warming brew and a rest before the day started properly. Alice brought her dad and younger brothers a steaming mug of tea.

"Alice! How pretty you look on this fine morning!" said Albert with a beaming smile.

"Why, thank you, kind sir!" she replied with a curtsey. "It's my birthday today, and momma has made me this new pinafore! I look like a proper lady!" she said with the most excited expression.

"Not for much longer, sis!" laughed John as he put his mug of strong tea down and raced after his sister, with his coal-stained hands outstretched in front of him.

Alice screamed and jumped off the boat, running down the towpath past Toby, much to the amusement of the boating community, who all smiled at her as she ran past.

"C'mon, you two!" shouted Albert with a proud smile upon his face. "There's work to be done John, boy, and chores to be done birthday or not! *Birthday presents...whatever next?*"

"What's that, Albert?" said Bert Wheelwright from the next barge.

"These young'uns with their birthdays!" replied Albert.

"Oh…I never had *time* for birthdays…come to think of it, I don't even know when mine is or how old I am, for that matter!" he said with a hearty laugh, his hands on both hips. Both men chuckled as a cloud of dust from the coal being loaded onto Bert's barge rolled over the canal and Bert disappeared within it.

Back inside the barge, Alice told her mother to take a breather whilst she cleaned up the dishes. When that was done, Alice placed the bed back into the bulkhead, making the 5' x 7' cabin into a small living room. When her mum had drunk her tea, she got on with starting on the men's dinners.

Albert, John and young James would eat their dinners on deck whilst Doris, Alice and Donald, who was only four, had theirs on the portable table in the cabin. But eating was a long way off, and there was much to do above and below deck. The coal had been filled into the hold and Leeds was half a day's pull for Toby on the Aire & Calder navigation. All the Watson children loved to go to the great Metropolis.

"What it must be like to wander along its cobbled streets and look at the fine gentlemen…" said Alice to her mum.

"Fine gentlemen, is it?" said Doris. "And what would *you* say, Alice, if you saw your *fine gentlemen?*"

"I don't know." Said Alice, and both women laughed together. In fact, laughter was the norm onboard their canal barge called 'Lightning'.

John Watson was daydreaming at the helm when his dad said, "A penny for 'em?"

John laughed. "You haven't got a penny!" They then both burst into laughter. "We live in a changing world, dad…" he said.

"How so?" replied Albert.

"There are magic lanterns in Leeds that don't need candles – they are powered by something called 'gas'".

A Switch in Time

"What nonsense!" scoffed Albert.

"It's true, dad! Alan Wheelwright told me – he's actually *seen* them!"

"You mean Bert's lad?" queried Albert.

"Well...he's a good lad, and he doesn't lie...but it just seems a bit *farcical* to me..."

"Can I have a quick look when we get there, dad? I will be back within the hour..." John said hopefully.

"After we have unloaded – but only an hour mind, you know your mother doesn't like you out late." Agreed Albert.

Albert looked up at the sky and thought '*I hope he gets to see his magic lamps...and it would be lovely if Alice could meet a nice young man...*'

"Oh, enough of this nonsense!" he quipped as his eyes focused back on the sky. He noticed what looked like a storm brewing, with a very strange cloud formation, over the centre of Leeds – which Albert now had at his bow.

As Albert gently eased the boat to its mooring alongside a dark and dusty mill on the canal bank, the wench was already making its way downwards with its grabber-pan open. With John on one end of the grabber and Albert on the other, they both began to push the two ends together. Before long the first load of coal was making its way skyward as the two very burly men tugged at the other side of the pulley. After this had been repeated many times, the hold was empty.

"Right then, dad, I'll be off then!" announced John.

"Have a care, John – I don't like the looks of that nasty cloud." Replied Albert

"A bit of rain won't bother me, dad!" laughed John as he leapt over the gunwhale and onto the canal bank.

John Paul Bernett

"John, stop!" cried Alice, "I'm coming with you! Mama said it was okay, dad!" as she kissed Albert and ran off before he time to reply.

"C'mon then sis, and keep up! We only have an hour!" replied John as they walked briskly along the towpath.

The two siblings both wondered what lay ahead. John's mind was full of technological marvels…Alice, on the other hand, was deep in thought about what she might say if she met a young gentleman…and would she blush if he enquired after her name?

Just as John and Alice reached the warehouses that lined the canal just before Leeds bridge, Alice let out a scream as she looked up, for the strange cloud formation was now *directly above them*. She stopped and threw her arms around John, burying her head in his chest, muffling her anguished cry. John glanced up and saw what could only be described as a *cloud*…swirling round in ever-decreasing circles…and it was heading straight for THEM. He tried to pull his sister to safety, but his old boots seemed *rooted* to the damp ground. With his arms firmly round his sister, he felt the first finger of this swirling cloud take his flat-cap from his head. He was now as afraid of this unworldly phenomenon as his poor sister, who was screaming quite freely. He wanted to join in with her – but he was a MAN now – so that was out of the question. There was now a deafening sound of wind screeching in their ears, with short bursts of lightning flashing through the tunnel that had formed around them. As they both stared up the tunnel-shaped whirling cloud wasn't going upward at all – the top of the cloud had come to rest upon the top floor of the adjacent warehouse! John and Alice's boots were no longer rooted to the ground…in fact, they were both slowly drifting inexorably towards the warehouse.

Alice screamed, "What's happening?"

"I don't know sis! Just hold on tight to me – I won't let you go!" answered John, his voice now distinctly quivering.

A Switch in Time

Tears were streaming down Alice's face and onto her new pinafore as she looked at the building growing ever-closer.

"Look!" shouted John. "I can see two people standing just in front of the building! They just seem to be floating near the top of it! He continued.

"I don't like it John – I want to go HOME!" sobbed Alice.

"Me too." Announced a now very-scared John Watson as he cuddled his sister ever-tighter. "They are coming towards us." He continued.

"What do they want with us? We haven't done anything wrong..." mumbled Alice into her brother's chest.

"I don't know sis – just close your eyes *really tight* – they might not see us."

CHAPTER THREE

Amanda Winters arrived back to a quiet house. The only light was emanating from the doorjamb of her husband's study. She let her shopping bags drop to the floor, and marched to the long slither of light shining through the door. As she was hoping that he would have started dressing for their daughter's party, she was *outraged* to find him in a deep slumber.

"ALFRED!" screamed Amanda.

He woke with a start and leapt out of his chair. "What's happened?" he quickly said.

"What has *happened? I have had to carry my own shopping in from the car whilst you were TAKING IT EASY!*" snapped Amanda.

Just like a pressure cooker that had finally accepted too much strain, Alfred exploded. *"THAT IS IT! I HAVE HAD ENOUGH!"* bellowed the man who had been under his family's thumb far too long. "Things are going to change round here...starting, *madam*, with YOU." He growled. Alfred Winters pushed past his dazed, open-mouthed wife and stormed out of his study into the lounge. Upon entering the room, he picked up the phone and called his daughter to deliver the *bombshell* that the *party was OFF*. Within seconds Amanda's mobile was ringing with the name '*Alicia*' flashing on its screen. Amanda answered the phone, and Alfred said, "Allow *me* to take your bags, DEAR."

Jamie and Freddie had spent most of the day outside, working on what they had decided was going to be the station ticket office. The day had been quite bright, until a strange cloud formation threatened to rain on them. Looking at the clock, Freddie alerted

A Switch in Time

Jamie to the time. Upon looking at said clock, Jamie shrugged his shoulders and said, "I don't suppose you will reconsider your decision, Fred..."

"Let me think...I can come with you and spend time with the *bitch from hell* and her *stomach-wrenching, spoilt, brainless, bimbo COW of a daughter*...or...stay here all night and work, mopping the floor with my TONGUE. It's the LATTER for me, matey!" was Fred's long, but very honest, reply.

"I'll take that as a *no,* then. By the way – will you check something for me?" asked Jamie.

"Sure. What do you want checking?" Freddie replied.

"Down in the cellar...behind the white brick...I've left some instructions for you to follow...I know it sounds dramatic, but in one hour's time, could you take that brick out of the wall and follow those instructions *exactly*?" asked Jamie, looking serious for a moment, but then smiling at his best friend.

Jamie had *no idea* why he had told his friend to do this – his subconscious mind must have taken over his thoughts for a short time.

"Uhh...okayyy...in one hour, remove the white brick, that has moss growing on it and very old mortar securing it in its place, so I can read the letter *you* have *left for me*...and do this in *one hour's time*..." he scoffed.

"I know...it sounds crazy, and I don't know why I'm saying it! But you *must be exactly as the letter says...your future happiness depends on it!"* replied Jamie quite seriously.

"O.K., one hour, and remove the brick, read about the future and then see you in a week, *'Mystic Meg'*...said Freddie.

"What?" said Jamie.

"You have got ME at it now! I mean, see you tomorrow!" replied Freddie, looking puzzled.

Back at the mansion, Amanda Winters, although still in a state of shock due to her husband's outrageous behaviour, tried to console her distraught darling little girl. Amanda agreed with her that her father was the *worst father in existence*.

"I will make SURE he changes his mind – don't forget, you are his *little princess...*" said a very-confident Amanda.

"This is the *worst birthday* anybody could possibly have! He had better *make up for it with something nice!* I hate him! I hate him! I hate him!" screamed Alicia.

"I know, my darling...but I'll make the old *skinflint* pay – just SEE if I don't!" announced a now battle-ready Amanda.

The battle, however, was short-lived, for as she entered the room where Alfred was, she noticed he had her credit and bank cards in one hand and a large pair of scissors in the other.

"I'm *glad* you're here to witness this! I've already CANCELLED Alicia's cards...and now, it's YOUR TURN!" said Alfred with aggression in his voice.

Amanda looked on in horror as the top blade of the scissors caught the light and glinted into her eyes as it sliced through the only thing she truly cared for. Her eyes rolled upwards as her legs gave way beneath her, and she fell to the ground. This was NOT the well-rehearsed faint that had gotten her so many nice things through the years – this was the *real deal.* As Alfred strolled over her prostrate form, he dropped the now-defunct cards on her ample but paid-for bosom. For what seemed the *first time in his life* – Alfred had *finally* stood up for himself! And it FELT GOOD.

With all the party guests cancelled, only one person was making his way to Alicia's apartment. In fact, it was the *only person who didn't want to go*. Remembering his phone had been switched off all afternoon, Jamie switched it back on as he arrived at Alicia's new building. He noticed once again strange clouds in the sky…only now they were swirling round the top of the building…he could see his sister out on the balcony looking down into the canal, and she was crying profusely. Jamie quickly entered the code for the door from the piece of paper his dad had given him. He opened the door and ran to the elevator, entering a second code for the penthouse. Soft music filled his ears as he was elevated upwards. The door to the apartment swished open and Jamie ran to the balcony, where he grabbed his sister and turned her around to face him.

"What's wrong, Alicia?" said Jamie.

"*Everything is RUINED. I wish I was MILES AWAY FROM HERE!* Screamed Alicia.

"Pull yourself together!" shouted Jamie. He had to shout, because the noise created by the winds was now *deafening*. With Alicia's head buried against his chest, he looked over his sobbing sibling into what had become a *whirlwind* behind her. Now the cloud formation was not in the sky at all – it was a tunnel, emanating from the towpath on the other side of the canal. Alicia's screams became louder as both hers and her brother's feet were wrenched from the balcony and into the vortex, which now had lightning flashing all around it. Once inside this swirling, flashing tunnel Jamie's grip on his sister grew tighter…he realized they were *not alone* in this vortex…there was what looked like a *man and woman, as helpless as they were, advancing towards them*. Jamie instinctively put Alicia behind him to offer some protection. As he did, the two sets of siblings converged and passed through each other like phantoms. Both Jamie Winters and John Watson caught each other's glance the instant both pairs of hugging siblings passed by one another. In an instant, they were back – one pair on the towpath, and the other on the balcony. The problem was…they were both on the wrong side of the canal…and the *wrong side of time*…

CHAPTER FOUR

Jamie and Alicia were the first to open their eyes – and what they saw made them both wince – the thing that stood out most was that the queer cloud formation was gone, and the area was heavy with smoke and grime...in fact, it was hard to make out the balcony where they had just stood a moment before. Heavy machinery could be heard from the building behind them and it was quite deafening. Alicia was the first to notice the clothes she was wearing.

"I LOOK AND SMELL HORRIBLE!" she shrieked.

"Be quiet! Don't draw attention to yourself! At least, not until I've worked out what's happened..." insisted Jamie.

"Okayyy *Mister know-it-all*! You find out what is happening; I'm going to get a bath and *burn these rags* that are polluting my body!" cried Alicia.

"Freddie is *absolutely right* about you! You are a *brainless bimbo!*"

As Jamie was talking to her, he grasped his sister's head with both hands and pointed it in the direction of her balcony. "Look...your apartment *isn't there anymore*...it's clearly a WAREHOUSE. Look around you, Alicia – everything is different! It's still *Leeds*...but not the Leeds we know! Just give me a minute or two to gather my thoughts..."

A Switch in Time

Alicia began to cry, and for the first time he could remember Jamie actually felt *sorry* for her. "C'mon sis, don't cry...I don't know what's happened yet, but I'll work it out." He said, as the first real thought came through the shock of what had just happened.

He noticed the canal boats, laden with coal. He saw the tall chimneys billowing black smoke into the sky. Most of all, he could hear the *swishing* and *whooshing* of *steam engines!* In the midst of all this, his brain was now telling him, no matter how OUTRAGEOUS it sounded, he and his sister were in the *19th century.*

John's grip on Alice tightened as his eyes slowly opened. Nothing could have prepared John Watson for the sight that lay before him. *'Are we dead...and in...heaven?'* he thought.

Alice opened her eyes, closely followed by her mouth, as she looked in AWE upon the sights her brain couldn't even *begin* to understand. Both John and Alice looked around whilst still holding tightly to each other. Alice was the first to speak.

"Is...is this...*heaven*, John?"

"I was just thinking that...let's go inside. I don't like it out here..." replied John.

They both let out a scream as they caught their reflections in the full-length mirror on the wall.

"*What am I wearing??*" gasped Alice as she saw the Prada gown that adorned her body. "And my hair...and face..." as she was wearing the latest hairstyle and makeup. "There is *paint* on my face...and *look at you! Your hair John...it's shining! And your clothes...we look like the QUEEN and her beloved Albert!* PLEASE tell me what's going on! I'm so scared, John...I want my mam!" she sobbed.

"Now I do know this...we aren't in heaven, because that was *not* a golden staircase...it was a scary whirly wind with lightning in it...and I learned *nothing* in the bible that said scary winds would carry you to heaven! Also...this can't be *hell*...because it's...too...nice! I wish our dad was here, cos he knows *everything about everything!"* said John.

"I can't see him knowing *anything* about this – because THIS IS MAGIC! And very soon, a fairy princess is going to fly in here and demand why am I wearing her clothes?" said Alice.

"What do YOU know of *fairy princesses*!" scoffed John.

"I know she won't take too kindly to you WEARING THE FAIRY KING'S CLOTHES, I can tell you THAT, my lad!" announced his elder sister.

"How can these clothes fit *fairies*...I'm thought of as a GIANT! I am five feet, eight and a half inches tall! I have to *bend* to get into some coal merchants doors! Fairy clothes WOULD NOT fit me!" replied John.

"*Of course they would fit, you silly man! They are MAGIC fairy clothes!"* announced Alice.

John smiled at his sister, and somehow, he knew their love would see them through.

After John and Alice's eyes adjusted to the *blinding* light of this new world, they let go of each other's hands. Alice tiptoed to the bedroom and gasped at the array of dresses and things she thought might be shoes – although she couldn't see any practical use for them. John looked out of the open glass doors and stepped through, back onto the balcony. It was difficult for his eyes to adjust to such *bright light*...and...to the sights on show in front of him. All of a sudden, he glimpsed something he knew! It was a factory...but it was...*clean*...and all the windows had *curtains!* He could see people inside, sitting, eating and drinking! Not *one* of them was working! There was no hustle and bustle outside...in fact, there was no coal, and no canal boats being loaded or unloaded! Everything looked *shiny,* and *new!* He KNEW he was looking at Leeds – he just couldn't understand what had happened to the only part of the great 'Metropolis' he had ever known. John Watson's mind didn't wander as easily as his sister's, so *magic* was *out of the question*. *'There has to be an answer to all this'* he thought…but try as he might, he could not fathom any answer *whatsoever*. It was at this point five sharp beeps could be heard, and the *whoosh* of an elevator door sliding open made both siblings turn towards the sound. John and Alice grabbed each other again in fright as an *enormous giant of a man* calmly stepped into the room.

On the other side of the canal, and of time, answers were coming thick and fast to Jamie. By looking at the skyline – or, what he could make of it – he was narrowing down to a decade either way of the year he and his sister were in. He had, in fact, narrowed it down to between 1840 and 1870, because Leeds Bridge hadn't been rebuilt yet, and the rebuilding of the famous bridge that spans the River Aire started in 1870. On the other side was a warehouse built in 1840. Jamie's mind was racing…but then he caught a glimpse of his sister. Alicia was *distraught*…she was sitting on the floor with her bosom pressed against her thighs, her arms wrapped round the front of her legs, sobbing like a little girl.

"Alicia…this isn't as bad as it seems…quite simply, you are having a *dream*…or in your case, I should say a *nightmare*. For some reason you have dragged me into it. Or…I am having a *wonderful dream* and have dragged *you* into *mine*. Either way, we will both wake up in the morning and everything will be back to normal." *'That should hold her for awhile…'* he thought.

"Do you *really* think so, Jamie?" asked Alicia.

Wow…thought Jamie…*that's the first time she has called me that in YEARS.* "Yes I do. Let's take a walk down the canal path, and see what we can find…" he said.

Jamie didn't know *why*, exactly, but he *knew* where he was going. As he passed a horse grazing upon clumps of grass on the towpath, he whispered, "*Hello Toby…*" in the horses' ear. As they approached the barge, Jamie realized he had *seen this boat before.* It was an old print on his father's office wall! He started to think, *this isn't Alicia's nightmare...this is a WONDERFUL dream!*

Reality soon hit home when a booming voice from the boat cried out, "Where have you two been! You told me you would only be an hour! And by my watch, you have been TWO! Your mother has been *beside herself* with worry! Now let's have you in, and you can explain to me *what happened!*" said an angry, but relieved, Albert Watson.

If what had happened up until now was mind-blowing to say the *least*...this was the *icing on the cake*! Because, although this was Alfred Watson from the 19th century, standing in front of James Albert Winters from the 21st century, Jamie was looking at his *father!* His looks...his voice...everything was the same!

"What's happening!" screamed Alicia.

"What's all this *screaming* about? What has happened to you, my girl?" shouted Doris as she took Alicia by the shoulders and shook her briskly. "Alice! Alice! Pull yourself *together!*" she continued. Alicia could not understand in any way what was going on. Why was her mother dressed in rags? Why were she and her father on this *ridiculous little boat*?

"WHAT'S HAPPENING!!" She screamed again. At this point, Doris slapped her across the face, and Alicia fainted into Jamie's arms.

At the other end of this *time rainbow*, a very scared John Watson looked up at this *towering* man that by now had walked over to them. Standing in front of his sister, he stuttered with a trembling voice, *"You will not get my sister, giant! You may be BIGGER than me, but I will protect her with MY LIFE!"*

The giant sat down on one of the sofas and calmly said, "Your sister is safe, as are you. Come and sit down...I have something to tell you both."

Gingerly John and Alice both sat down, although they never let go of each other's tight grip. With a smile on his face, the giant started to speak.

"How am I going to begin this?" he said with a chuckle. "It's time for introductions...my name is Freddie Chambers, and I know that you two lovely people are John and Alice Watson...and one thing is *for certain*...I am NOT giant, I am only 6'5" tall. In my time, many people are my size, and some are taller than I!"

"*So...you are not going to eat us for your tea?*" said Alice in a quivering voice.

"No I am NOT!" said Freddie with a chuckle in his voice.

"Can you tell us what has happened?" enquired John.

"There isn't an easy answer to that question, my friend...and you are not here because of something that you have done. You are good people, and when you go back, you probably won't remember *any* of this. You have *swapped places* with another brother and sister, and the sister is definitely *not* as nice as you are, Alice." Said Freddie.

"You said, when we get back...could you tell us when that will be, sir?" asked John.

"For you guys, not too long at all. For one of the other two...it will seem *endless*..." replied Freddie. "They are both going to live *your lives* for a week...for *your* counterpart, John, it will be a *dream*...but for yours, Alice, it will be a *nightmare*."

"I don't understand *counterpart*, sir..." said John.

"Oh...I'm sorry, John. My friend Jamie has taken your place, back in *your time*, and his horrible excuse for a sister has taken *its* place of your dear sister." Explained Freddie.

"But won't our mam and dad worry where we are?" asked John anxiously.

"Now *this* is where it gets *really complicated*...I mean, really hard to *understand*...all of this will seem like only an hour has gone by to them, so everything will be the *same* when you return." Said Freddie.

"I wish I was back already!" said Alice.

"When you said *back in your time*...does that mean we are now in a time that comes...*after ours*?" asked John Watson.

"Yes John. It's called the *future*...but please, don't question me about it. Because we all know what trouble *Marty McFly* got into over it..."

"Marty McFly?" was John's answer.

"That's *exactly* what I mean. You don't know about these things...so how can I tell you?" answered Freddie, seemingly digging himself into a hole.

"If you tell us, then we will *understand*." Said Alice.

"Yes...but if I were to tell you about *steam engines*, for instance, you might go back and invent them...before they were invented...and what would *that* do to the space-time continuum? It's just too *frightening* to think of!" replied Freddie, whose hole was getting deeper by the second.

"You *know* about steam engines?? I want to learn about them! You *must* tell me all you know! And what of *lamps without candles*??" said a now very-excited John Watson.

"Now let's STOP RIGHT THERE." Said Freddie. "This is *exactly what I am talking about!* You *cannot* find out about these things *from me!* I'm only here to see that *you* stay safe whilst you are here!" he continued.

John Watson got up and stared out of the window onto a brave new world, and said, "The answers to *all of my questions* are out there...and I have to stay *in here*...*knowing that!* Surely sir, if you only *knew* how much I have longed for these kind of answers,

A Switch in Time

you would impart to me some small amount of knowledge…even if it was only up to when I came from!"

Freddie sat back, and scratching his chin he said, "I will check on my history…what date was it when you were last there?"

"It's *my birthday!*" said Alice, smiling again.

"Many happy returns of the day!" said Freddie.

"What does that mean?" asked Alice.

"Oh…it's just my silly way of saying I'm glad that it's your birthday! So…what year is it?"

"It's 1849…" answered John.

"I will see what I can do…but only up to 1849. Now – what do you two like to eat?"

Back on the coal barge, Alicia had come round from her faint. "I'm still here…on this horrible boat!" she cried.

"Alicia…your faints are *not* going to work here." Said Jamie as he looked down at the tear-stained face of his sister. "Remember, it's just a *dream*…we have to do as we are told here, but it's only for a short time. Then, you can go back to being a *dumb bimbo* with your *sickening friends.*"

Remembering it was just a dream made her calm down, just as Doris said, "Now you are back in the land of the living, you can get those *pots washed.*"

Begrudgingly, Alicia made her way to the large bowl with the teatime pots and pans in it. "THIS WATER IS FREEZING COLD!" she screamed.

"Do what you *always do*…put water in it from the kettle, you stupid girl!" said Doris as she looked at Jamie and gave him a wink.

At first, Jamie looked puzzled. Looking over at Albert, he noticed he wore a smile on his face, too.

"Come upstairs, lad, I've some news for thee…" said Albert with a grin.

Both men went on deck, and Albert lit his tobacco. A plume of thick gray smoke filled the air as he sucked on his favourite pipe.

In the cabin, Doris noticed Alicia's nails and said, "What has happened to your *fingernails*, my girl? Put your hands on my cutting board!"

"And *precisely WHAT do you think you're GOING TO DO?*" screamed Alicia.

"I will show you my girl." Said Doris as she retrieved a large knife from a little drawer. "And you *raise your voice to me one more time, young lady, I will SLAP YOU SO HARD YOUR TEETH WILL RATTLE!*" she continued.

Doris Watson placed Alicia's hand on the cutting board, so that the back of her hand faced downwards, then she chopped off the jewelled, perfectly manicured tips from each nail. Alicia tried to struggle, but her thin 21st century frame was *no match* for the hard-working frame of Doris Watson, and very soon, four-hundred pounds worth of nail extensions had been thrown into the fire. Once again, Alicia Winters fainted.

Now on the canal bank, Albert, through the pipe smoke, was talking to Jamie Winters.

"So then, lad, what's this here *future* of yours like?"

Jamie just stood there with his mouth open, not knowing what to say.

Albert laughed and said, "It's alright, lad. Things are happening *too fast* around here for me to worry about what's going to happen when I'm *dead and gone.*"

"But…but…but…how *do you know*?" stuttered Jamie.

"I don't know, young James." Said the truthful boatman. I saw a strange cloud formation as John and Alice were leaving, and at the same time I heard a voice inside my head. It was likened to a *familiar family voice*...but I couldn't remember who...something about their *spoiled family*. Well I don't know how you can *spoil* a family, or what that means...then a *different voice* predicted your arrival...and that my kids *would be safe*...and that you and your *strange sister* would be coming here for a week. She isn't used to hard work, is she?" continued Albert, taking another drag on his pipe.

Jamie was grateful for this turn of events, and said, "I'm sure that your children will be safe. I don't know what is happening...I have a feeling my sister is getting *brought down to Earth*. Do you mind if I go and search out an engineering factory?"

"You're just like my own son John, his head is full of all this new nonsense. Yes, you can set off in the morning...but be back here within a week...or you will be *stuck here*, and I might not get my John back!" said Albert as they returned to the boat.

"I will be back *each night*...and I *promise*, I will be no trouble to you." Said Jamie with a broad smile on his face.

When both men returned, Alicia was just coming round from her faint. When she saw her brother, she shouted, "WILL YOU TAKE A LOOK AT THE WAY *SHE* HAS BUTCHERED *MY NAILS*?" She lifted up both her hands in disgust.

"Your nails would've *gotten in the way of your work* how you had them...and *just think* how much it would have *cost you* to get them cut! Doris has saved you a few hundred quid!" Jamie quipped.

"WORK?!" Screamed Alicia.

"Yes!" said Albert. "Work! You had better get an early night, because you will be up at five in the morning..." he continued.

"FIVE??!!" Alicia screamed again.

"She doesn't use a lot of words, does she?" said Albert, looking at Jamie.

"You're using words *she doesn't understand.*" Replied Jamie with a smile.

Alicia stamped her foot hard on the boat floor and *demanded* to be shown to her room.

"You are *standing in it.*" Replied Doris.

"Where is *everyone else* sleeping?" enquired Alicia.

"Same place, where else…silly girl?" retorted Doris.

"I am NOT SLEEPING IN THE SAME ROOM AS *YOU PEOPLE*!!" said a defiant Alicia.

"Now I HAVE HAD ENOUGH! ANYMORE OF THIS AND YOU ARE GOING OVER MY KNEE, GIRL!" boomed Albert.

"YOU JUST *TRY IT* AND I'LL HAVE YOU ARRESTED!" she screamed.

"That's it, my girl!" and with that, Albert grabbed hold of Alicia, sat himself down and placed her over his knee.

"DON'T YOU *DARE!*" she screamed again, as she felt her dress get pulled over her head and then the first *thunderous clap* on her naked bottom of Albert's right hand. She felt the slap again and *again* until the cheeks of her bottom were red raw. Albert stood up and stood Alicia upright again. Tears were streaming down her bewildered face. She looked at Jamie in disbelief…that he could allow such an *atrocity* to take place without lifting a finger to help! She felt scared…and *alone*…but most of all, she felt *desecrated.*

A Switch in Time

John Paul Bernett

CHAPTER FIVE

Freddie Chambers scratched his head as he was checking again what had happened in British history up until the mid-nineteenth century. The food thing was easy…it was all one-pot meals with *very little* meat…maybe the odd rabbit…it was useful to Freddie that Jamie's history case work from university was in folders at his flat. After going through Jamie's notes, he realized why he'd been awarded an honour's degree.

Back at Alicia's penthouse, Alice and John had begun investigating their new surroundings.

"None of this is real, sis…" said John.

"I know John…but it's the first time I've ever been in a *palace*…" replied Alice.

"Alice…it's the first time you've been in a *building*!" laughed John.

"Look how *big* everything is here!" said Alice, whose voice now had an edge of *excitement* about it for the first time since their strange arrival. Just then, Alice noticed a fruit bowl. It was in a part of the house that she couldn't understand. Biting into a crisp Golden Delicious apple, she said, "I wonder what this room is for, John?"

A Switch in Time

Her brother joined her in the kitchen and said, "I can't imagine *what goes on in here…*"

As far as the two siblings from the 19th century were concerned, it might as well have been the bridge from a space shuttle, because *none* of the items in that room resembled a kitchen that they had *ever* witnessed. It was about this time that Freddie Chambers arrived back. As the elevator doors swished open, heralding hisreturn, the Victorian siblings instantly held onto each other again in a scared embrace.

"You two are going to have to get used to that entrance while you are here…" quipped Freddie, "Or I'm going to have to use the stairs!

"So you are *still using stairs* in this wonderful age you live in?" asked John.

"Yes…we still use stairs…mainly as fire escapes, bedrooms, that sort of thing…" replied Freddie, instantly putting his hands over his mouth. "STOP ASKING ME QUESTIONS LIKE THAT!" he continued.

Freddie made his way into the kitchen. John took his sister by the shoulders. *"That's my way out of here…and into this modern world! Just think what I could LEARN, sis! I could have a glimpse…into the FUTURE! I will find these stairs and escape for an hour or two when Freddie leaves again!"* said a rather excited John.

"No, John!" screamed Alice.

John placed his hand over her mouth and whispered, "Shush! I will be back before you know! You are *very safe* here and there is *nothing* to fear!"

Soon, the wondrous smell of rabbit stew began wafting in from the strange room, filling the entire area with the smell of *home*. All thoughts of escape left John's mind for a moment as his empty stomach took over his power of thought.

"Go sit at the table!" shouted Freddie as he marched in from the kitchen with two steaming bowls of rabbit stew in his hands.

"How can you have that ready *so fast*?" enquired an excited Alice.

"Ahhh...the wonders of the Micro...whoa! This is IMPOSSIBLE!" exclaimed poor Freddie, failing at every opportunity to keep the future from his guests.

"*More magic!*" exclaimed Alice.

Freddie just shook his head and gave his wards their evening meal. The two siblings tucked into their food without a sound, just eager enthusiasm.

When the meal was over, all three moved into the living room and began talking about the history of their wonderful country up to the late 1850s. John knew some of what Freddie was teaching him, and this impressed Freddie. John's interest and knowledge of the late *Matthew Murray* was surprising to Freddie, because like a lot of people, Freddie had the misunderstanding that Victorian meant mostly poverty, disease and *ignorance*. John began telling Freddie about his father, and how he got started on the canals.

"My father believes there can be no greater power than a *horse* – he doesn't realize that the new engines which are being built *right here in Leeds* have the power of *many horses*...my friend has seen one in action...and he said it was the best, and *most frightening*, thing, he had ever seen. I want to go work on the railways...I want to be an engineer!"

"Don't be *silly,* John! You have to stay and work the barge!" laughed Alice.

"I know..." John replied with a faraway look in his eyes.

"You can be *whatever you want to be*..." replied Freddie.

"Is that the *modern* way of thinking, Mr. Chambers? Because that is far from the truth in *my day*...only MONEY gets you where

A Switch in Time

you want where we are from…and we don't have any. My life is on the *canal*…and engineering is for my *private thoughts*." Explained John.

Freddie instantly thought of *Alicia*…and how money had indeed gotten her everything she had wanted. He had always hated Alicia, but after hearing John lament upon something he could never be, his hatred of that spoilt bitch grew to *epic proportions*. He hoped she was getting was she deserved in the 19th century…

CHAPTER SIX

It was around 5 a.m. when Alicia's *worst ever* night of sleep was ended by Doris Watson shaking her arm.

"C'mon girl, time to start…"

Alicia was disoriented and didn't realize where she was for a moment, but as the smell of that *tiny* room filled her nostrils, and the awareness that she wasn't alone on the makeshift bed hit her, it all came flooding back. Tears welled up in her eyes as her bottom lip began to quiver.

"Don't start all that *crying* again…you have *work* to do!" said Doris.

"I need to go to the bathroom…" whimpered Alicia.

"Bathroom? Such words I've never heard! What are you *talking about*, girl?" replied Doris.

At this point, Jamie had awakened and pointed to the bucket in the corner of the room. Doris saw Jamie point to the bucket and said, "If that's the bathroom, you can go *empty it* because it's nearly full."

A Switch in Time

The look of *absolute horror* on Alicia's face as she stared towards the bucket full of *human waste* would have won an Oscar if she had been an actress.

"Go on then...do what you have to and then throw it overboard...that's a good girl, we have breakfast to make! This is what you will be doing from *now on*." Doris continued.

"I'm not doing it *here*...in front of everybody!" sputtered Alicia.

"Well go do it *outside*, then...but watch the *rats*...they are very hungry at this time of year."

At that point, Alicia just wanted to *die*. She couldn't take anymore. Albert had also been awakened from his slumber and said, "If you don't want the same as you got last night, you'd better *do as your told*...because if a little *slap* on your behind didn't set you straight, I will take my BELT to you!"

Jamie and Alicia looked at the four-inch-wide belt around Albert's girth and then looked at each other. Alicia picked up the bucket with both of her hands and struggled up the steps and onto the deck with it. She climbed off the boat and then reached back over to pick it up again. Unfortunately for her, she didn't get ahold of it properly and it dropped back onto the deck. The bucket stayed upright, but some of its contents splashed up onto her face and clothes. Inwardly she wanted to *scream out loud*...but was beginning to fear Albert and did not want to incur his rage again. Quietly sobbing to herself, she lifted her dress and sat her tiny pampered bottom onto the cold wet bucket and did what she had to do. Upon finishing, her stomach wrenched and the small amount of food that was in it was ejected into the canal.

When Alicia returned, Jamie and Albert were having their breakfast. Jamie then stood putting on his jacket and said, "I'm going to get off now."

Albert wished him luck and said, "Remember boy, *six days*..."

"I'll remember." Said Jamie.

Alicia screamed out, *"Please don't leave me here, Jamie! I beg of you, don't leave me here!"*

"You are going to have to sort everything out yourself...without the use of money, bank cards, people running errands for you...*or your Blackberry...*"

"There are no blackberries this time of year..." said Albert.

"I know." Said Jamie as he went to give his sister a kiss on the cheek, but then decided not to when he saw what was on it.

As he left he looked back at Alicia and gave her a reassuring smile. "I will see you soon." He told her. With that parting glance, Jamie was gone, and Alicia was alone with these strange, out of touch people.

She pulled herself together and said, "OK. Obviously, this is some sort of *penance* that I must *endure* for reasons that I cannot think of..."

"Let me stop this fine speech you are giving, Miss *Alicia*..." said Albert.

"*I was under the impression you thought I was ALICE!*" she snapped.

"You couldn't *hold a candle* to that sweet child of ours..." retorted Albert.

"In *what way* is your 'Alice' so *different to me*...apart from her *hygiene*, that is?"

"What is *hygiene*?" asked Doris.

"I MEAN, she wears FILTHY CLOTHES, DOESN'T BATHE AND SHE *SMELLS!*" snarled Alicia.

"WE WORK IN A CONSTANT CLOUD OF COAL DUST. THAT IS *WORK* THAT YOU SMELL ON HER CLOTHES...A THING YOU KNOW *NOTHING ABOUT!* ALICE IS A *USEFUL PART* OF THIS BOAT CREW! Ask yourself this, young lady...have you ever been useful to ANYONE for ANYTHING in your ENTIRE LIFE?!!" Albert awaited a reply.

Alicia just stood there trying to think of a time...of a single *instant*...when she had been *useful* to someone. The realization was, not *one single instance* came to mind of a time when she had been of use to *anybody*. What Albert just said is what the people back in her own century *really thought of her*. Alicia began to cry...not like before...these tears were *real*, as the depressing thought of how people really saw her hit home.

This time Albert didn't scold her for crying...he simply looked at Doris and gave her a wink.

Albert went topside and stood at the helm thinking of his own daughter in that *horrid place* that had spawned such a self-centered creature, and wished for her back, along with her brother. Alicia looked at Doris, mapping the lines of her aged face and the dark shadows beneath her eyes, and wondered about living a life in a time where growing old was the norm. Sadness fell upon her and she couldn't work out *why*. For the first time in her precious life, she *pitied* someone. She then looked around at what Albert and Doris called 'home'. She tried to conceive *how they could be happy* living an existence without money, possessions, going out to dinner with friends, a new car every year...these people were PROUD people...proud of their little business, their horse...but most of all their *children*. Alicia recalled the last telephone conversation she had had with her mother, complaining that her father was *horrible*...and her mother saying she would *make him pay*. Alicia just stood and hung her head.

As Albert stared into the distance over the empty hold of his canal barge, he was brought back into sharp focus by a tap on his shoulder. Startled, he spun around. To his *amazement*, Alicia stood there with a pint pot of tea, which she offered to him.

"What's this?" said Albert.

"Tea?" replied Alicia.

"Thank you Alicia...now go thank Doris for me..."

"Doris is having a nap. I made it for you." Replied Alicia.

"There is hope for you yet..." he said with some trepidation as to the contents of his favourite mug. "All this is as *strange to me as it is to you. I don't know why you are here, but HERE you ARE.* All I know is, while you are here you have to do as we do." Said Albert in a stern, but gentle, voice.

As they were talking, three young children walked past the barge, and all of them looked at Alicia...their *gaunt, dirty faces...their rags that were loosely tied together with bits of string...their bare feet* seemed to affect Alicia, and she turned her head away. She recalled the boots she had just bought, and realized the amount of money she had paid for them would have been *enough to have clothed HUNDREDS of these poor children*. She was finding pity in her up-until-now closed heart. She began to think about her penthouse, and the tiny space Albert and Doris had brought their family up in. She was trying to work out how they could be *happier* than she...then suddenly it came to her. *My happiness relies upon POSSESSIONS...and this is the SUM OF MY LIFE...*

"What are 'possessions'?" enquired Albert.

Alicia, not realizing she had just spoken out loud, gave a little cough of embarrassment and said, "They are things that you collect...and they make you feel...*good*...about yourself."

"I see..." Albert said. "And if you do not have these *possessions* of yours...you cannot feel good about yourself?"

Alicia hung her head, not knowing how to answer, for here was a man with *nothing at all*, as happy as a man could be...and the *worst thing was...she could not understand it AT ALL.*

Albert continued, "You see, young Alicia, the only possession *anyone* needs is the love of their family! And you don't need to

A Switch in Time

be a *king* or a *fine gentleman* to have that, because the thing that is most important in life is FREE!"

"All you need is *love*...eh?? John Lennon preached that and look what happened to him..." Alicia's words covered up the turmoil she now felt inside, recalling all the bad things she had said to her father...and yet he just kept on *loving her*. Worst of all she was thinking about her *mother*...and the stark realization that she was a *carbon copy* of her.

"Dunno a *John* Lennon...but I DO know Arthur Lennon! He is a good man – works the other end of the Leeds/Liverpool canal! Good singing voice, as I recall..."

Just three-quarters of a mile away, Jamie was standing in front of the building that in the 21st century he *owned*. He was amazed by its *newness*...and immediately began sketching it on the empty notepad in John's coat that he was wearing. He noticed the railway line actually ran *through* the building and not along the *outside* as it seemed to do in his day. He kept drawing until someone came out and inquired about his actions.

"I'm looking for work." Said Jamie.

"You'd better come inside, lad." Said the gentleman.

As the two men entered what looked like the offices, Jamie noticed a painting on the wall of someone he recognized...it was a likeness of *Matthew Murray*! The man who had brought him inside noticed Jamie looking at the painting and said, "He was a *brilliant* engineer!"

"I know...I've studied him well." Said Jamie.

"Have you now? You don't look the educated type to me...judging by your appearance, I was about to set you on in the boiler room shovelling coal!" said Jack Hawkins, the Works Manager.

"I have studied engineering in *history*." Said Jamie.

"*History?* What we are doing is new and exciting, lad! I'm not talking about building *wooden ships and haycarts*...we are building ENGINES that are POWERED by STEAM!" exclaimed a puzzled Jack.

"Umm...*Modern History...*" Said Jamie, realizing his mistake. "I learned Modern History at University, Sir!" he continued, instantly realizing the hole he was digging for himself was getting deeper by the minute.

"Hmm...University...and the *father* who sent you to University also sent you to me looking like a *ragamuffin*?" inquired Mr. Hawkins sarcastically.

"I want to be an engineer, Sir...I want a hands-on experience of using steam as a power source!" replied Jamie.

"Okay, Mister University-Man...show me what you have learned in your...*history class...*" said Jack Hawkins.

Jamie saw some drawings of a steam locomotive on the desk. He quickly looked over them, and then proceeded to name all the component parts of the working engine. He gave a full description of the steam pistons, and was moving onto the boiler when Jack Hawkins stopped him.

"How do you know all this at your age? An *awful lot* of what you just told me is *priveledged information*...where did you learn it from?"

"As I *said*, Sir, at University...I dress like this because my family has fallen upon hard times..." replied Jamie.

"In that case, I will give you a start, young man. Now, first things first – what's your name?"

Thinking quickly, Jamie answered, "John Watson." He didn't want *his* name showing up on historical records.

"Well, John Watson...you can start next Monday!"

The Works Manager was interrupted by Jamie.

"I can start right now, if that's okay, the *sooner the better for me!*"

"*Keen eh?* I like that! First, we will see if you can *work*. If I am going to take on an apprentice, I want to see what you are *made of*. Come with me…" said Jack.

Both men climbed down the step ladder into the building's cellar. The cellar was cold and damp, and illuminated by three candles. Normally, it would have taken Jamie's eyes a while to adjust, but the dim light of this era made it so there was hardly ever bright light due to the smoke and soot emanating from the tall chimneys of Hunslet and Holbeck. As the two men walked towards a wall that needed some attention, Jack Hawkins said, "What do you know of *bricks and mortar*?"

"I can lay bricks." Was Jamie's confident reply.

"There you go, then, lad – fix that wall today, and if you do it right, you begin your apprenticeship with me, and we will put that University knowledge of yours to some practical use!"

After Jack Hawkins had left the cellar, Jamie surveyed the wall to see what was needed. He knew he could do the job, because this part of the wall was still standing back in his time. The first thing he did was to write the note that Freddie would read on that fateful night of his sister's birthday. Then, as he laid the bricks one after another, he reached the part that needed the painted brick…and to his delight, there, laying on the floor, was a *single white glazed brick*, which he placed into the wall that he was building and carried on until the cellar wall, albeit six foot square, was finished. Then he made his way back up the ladder knowing that the letter for Freddie was safely placed behind the white brick for him to read 164 years or so later.

Back at the canal, it was *all systems go* as Albert had decided it was time to do some much-needed repairs to the barge. Assembling his crew, he was surprised to see Alicia was as willing as the rest of them! He set young James on with polishing the horses harnesses and to groom Toby. Doris already had the mop and bucket ready in preparation of the cleaning duties. She handed one of the mops and the bucket to Alicia.

"Do you know how to use one of these?" she asked.

"I have the basic idea..." said Alicia.

"Right then! Doris portside, Alicia starboard! *That's the right-hand side...*" said Albert with a smile.

The two women set to their tasks. Alicia was *amazed* at how industrious Doris was for her age. She thought of her own mother, and wondered what *she* would do in a case like this. She quickly realized her mother would simply break down and cry. She also realized that that was exactly what *she had been doing* since she had arrived there. This was a pivotal moment for Alicia. She already *knew* she was a carbon copy of her mother, and realized *then and there* that she HAD to change. Alicia set about her cleaning duties. Although Doris was way in front of her and her arms were aching and painful, she began to feel something that she did not recognize. She was actually feeling *proud* of something that she was doing. This was *hard toil*...which, until she had arrived at this period in time, she had *never known*. Albert had climbed into the hold and started checking for weak spots. Tapping with his hammer, he made his way down the long sides of his pride and joy, checking for differences in the sounds his hammer was making. Alicia had now rolled up her sleeves, and was working harder than she had ever done in her priveledged life. The result of this work was plain to see...she also understood why Doris had removed her fingernail extensions. The very fact that Alicia wasn't worrying about her *precious fingernails* made it easier to take on this work! Her unmade-up face was now sporting a *wry smile*.

"A penny for them, lass..." said Albert.

"I was just thinking about what my friends back home would think of me now, if they could see me." Replied Alice.

"Never you mind what your friends would think...I can tell you *this*...your family would be DAMN PROUD OF YOU!" encouraged Albert.

"I am sure my *father and brother* would be proud of me...but my mother would be disgusted at the fact that I had 'lowered' myself to doing such a *menial task*." She replied.

"Seems to me it should have been your *mother* accompanying you, and not your brother..." pondered Albert.

Alicia let out a shriek of laughter and said, "My GOD! The *very thought of my pampered mother being here RIGHT NOW and doing what I AM DOING*...well, it's just...UNTHINKABLE! The thing I don't understand is why my *brother* is here. I know now *exactly* why I am here...but Jamie is not like me at all! He is a good man who has never lusted after money or influential friends in his entire life!"

"Maybe it isn't what *Jamie* has done in his time that is the reason he is here...I think he is here to help somebody in this time. Don't ask me why...but I think he is here to help my son John..." said a thoughtful Albert.

"How can *Jamie* help *John*, when John isn't here?" asked Alicia.

"I think Jamie is starting the life that John wants, but didn't know how to go about it..." explained Albert.

The conversation came to a halt at the arrival of Doris bearing three pots of steaming-hot tea.

"Now then, you two – I see I am not stopping you both from working! Standing there chatting like there is nothing to do!" laughed Doris. "What's happened to James?"

"The last I saw of him, he was galloping down the towpath with Toby..." said Alicia.

"I don't know...all that lad wants to do is *play*..." said Doris shaking her head and going after her wayward son.

This was another moment that made Alicia stop and think, for James was just a *boy*...and in her world, it would be perfectly *natural* for a boy his age to be out playing. She had noticed that none of the children she had seen on the canal side had actually been *playing*...they were all working, and this made her feel sad. It also reminded her again of how spoilt she was in her previous life...and how if she ever got back there, things would change...starting with her *mother*. Alicia had seen Albert and Doris sitting on a makeshift chair *laughing together*, and she tried to think, when was the last time she had seen *her parents* sitting together, laughing. Oh, how things were going to be different when...*if*...she ever got home.

Once the tea had been drunk, it was all hands on deck again and back to work. Albert was laughing at the sight of young James being brought back to the boat by his ear, with his mother saying, "I'll give you running off with Toby, when there is work to be done, my lad! Now get hold of that bucket and come with me!"

"What did you do when you were a young'un, lass?" inquired Albert.

"I was at school with all the rest of the children..." replied Alicia.

"Bloody hell! How long do you stay at school in your time?" asked Albert.

"Until we are 16 – we can then stay until we are 18, if we want..." informed Alicia.

"Eighteen!! I had been *working* twelve years by the time I was eighteen!" said Albert.

"Yes...but not *everything* about this age is good, Albert..." said Alicia.

"That's the first time you've called me Albert! We are definitely making progress!" he said, placing his flat cap back on his head.

Alicia just gave him a knowing smile. The family resumed their work and continued through until it was dinner time.

It was lunchtime in another part of town…and Jamie realized suddenly that he had not brought anything to eat with him. This, of course, did not dampen his enthusiasm, because he was now climbing the ladder back into the actual Works. He saw Jack Hawkins standing by one of the machines, talking to a worker. Making his way towards him, the Works Manager pointed to his office, so Jamie diverted his walk towards Jack Hawkins' office. A minute or two later, he was joined in the office by the Works Manager.

"Now then, lad…I hope you've finished your work, because you've been down there awhile." Jack said.

"Indeed I have, Sir!" was Jamie's reply.

"Good lad! We shall check your work after lunch. I did notice you weren't carrying a bag of any kind when you arrived this morning…have you not brought any lunch?"

"I'm afraid I never *thought* of lunch – my head was too full of finding a work position for me to think of food."

"It's your *lucky day*, then! Because my wife has packed me up *far too much lunch* for me to manage by myself! Would you care to join me?"

Being powerful hungry after his brick-laying, Jamie replied, "How very kind of you to offer, Sir – I would be most grateful!"

"Politeness…I *do like that*! I don't get enough of it from the usual people that I set on here! I think I'm going to *enjoy teaching you*…and unlike most I have met whilst I've been the Works Manager, I think you will *profit* from my teaching…you appear to be different from the rest in your age bracket. I can't quite *put my finger on it*…but you are *different*…" said Hawkins.

"Thank you, Sir! I will do my best not to let you down!" said Jamie.

The two men finished their lunch of bread, cheese and ale and made their way back down into the cellar. Jack Hawkins looked closely at Jamie's new brick work, and inquired after the white brick that was laying right in the centre of it. Jamie explained that he had found it on the floor, and had assumed that it had been in the wall in the first place. Jack Hawkins nodded his head and patted Jamie on the back, saying, "Excellent work, young lad! Your apprenticeship will start tomorrow, as agreed! I will see you first thing in the morning! I cannot abide lateness, so be here for half-past seven and not a minute later!" said Jack as he bid Jamie good day.

Half an hour later, Jamie returned to the barge and asked, "What is happening here, then?"

"I thought while you were doing what you need to be doing, I would use the time to make some much-need repairs." Announced Albert.

"What a good idea, Albert! I don't start until tomorrow morning, so I am at your disposal for the rest of the day!" offered Jamie.

"I was hoping you'd be able to help me!" said Albert.

Jamie smiled at Albert and said, "Of course I will." Jamie caught sight of his sister...*working*. "Is that *you,* Alicia?" Jamie now doubted his sense of sight as he saw Alicia emerging from a cloud of dust rubbing her nose and smiling.

"Very funny!" coughed Alicia. "Why are you back so early?" she continued.

"Because I don't start properly until tomorrow morning..." he replied, still looking bemused. "Have you been *working*, Alicia?" he continued.

"I have been working *very hard all morning*...and I will have you know that I hurt *all over*!" she retorted.

"And a good job she's doing, too!" said Albert.

Jamie once again looked upon his sister with different eyes...she was covered from head to toe in coal dust. She wasn't complaining...and she was *smiling* about it.

45

A Switch in Time

"Well done, Alicia! I'm proud of you!" said Jamie.

"Thank you, Jamie." Was Alicia's reply. For the first time she as well saw her brother with different eyes.

"This patting on the back is all very well and good – but it's *not* getting the job done!" announced Albert.

CHAPTER 7

Back in the 21st century, Freddie Chambers had left the penthouse to go do some shopping. This was what John Watson had been waiting for! He took hold of his sister's hands, looked her in the eyes and said, "I will be back before you know it, sis!"

"No!" cried Alice. "It's *too dangerous*! What if you get *lost?*" she continued.

"I know this part of Leeds, and I won't wander past it." John reassured his frightened sibling.

With that, John made for the stairwell and down the steps to the bottom of the building. As he walked to the door that led to freedom, it just opened with a *whooshing* noise...this startled John, but then he remembered the whooshing door that Freddie used to get in and out of the 'palace'. Stepping outside, he was *free in a world of technology*...having escaped the confines of the penthouse, he set off at a quick pace, not knowing quite where he was going. Just as John was settling down to the bright, tall buildings and all the people rushing about him, the *scariest noise he had ever heard seemed to be splitting his eardrums.* The sound was emanating from the sky...nervously, he looked up – and there in the sky was a *dragon*...just hovering above him!

A Switch in Time

John screamed out loud, turned around and ran back to the apartment building, faster than he had ever run in his *life*. The police helicopter flew off in the opposite direction. As luck would have it, someone was entering the apartment building just as John arrived. He pushed straight past him and rushed up the stairwell without stopping, and was through the unlocked door and straight into the arms of his beloved sister.

"Whatever's the matter, John? I've never seen you like this before!" asked his anxious sister.

"I was *nearly eaten by a DRAGON*! And I think I knocked somebody over downstairs!" he replied.

"I *told you* this is a *magic place* – it's *too dangerous to go out there!*" instructed Alice.

"Don't you worry sis! I won't be going back out there!" he replied.

The door to the penthouse whooshed open and a rather rattled Freddie Chambers entered.

"Are you alright?" asked Alice.

"No I am not...some damned *hooligan* knocked me over when I was opening the door outside! I didn't see who it was, because he was through the lobby and into the stairwell before I knew what was happening!" replied Freddie.

John and Alice looked at each other and burst into laughter.

"I'm glad you two think it's funny! Anyway, John, I have some books about Victorian history that you and I can go over this evening...and perhaps, Alice, I will draw you a bath so that you can relax!"

"What is a *bath?*" asked a puzzled Alice.

"Come with me, and I will show you..." Freddie said.

Freddie and Alice walked towards the bathroom. John began looking at the photographs in the books.

Once inside, Alice's mouth opened to a gape as she stared at the beautifully tiled Italian walls and floor. Placed in the middle of this *opulent room* was a grand, stand-alone bathtub, which Freddie began to fill. Alice walked over to see what he was doing. When she got to the tub, she saw the crystal-clear water that suddenly bubbled into a frenzy! Freddie put the bubble bath bottle down, placed his hands into the bubbles and then placed some on Alice's nose.

"Now, Alice, the water is just the right temperature for you to get in and soak in these lovely bubbles…just take off your clothes and climb in!"

Before Freddie could leave, she had instantly removed her clothes, took hold of Freddie's steadying hand and stepped into the awaiting bathtub. Freddie had *never seen such a vision of female beauty in his LIFE.* Her femininity was so estranged from what his time period thought of as 'beauty'…whilst he stared in awe, John entered the room, brandishing a book and a very excited facial expression.

"Look at this, sis! It's a *steam engine!*" blurted John, putting the book right in front of his elder sister's face.

"That looks exciting John!" she said.

"It's what I want to do, Alice!" replied her excitable brother.

Freddie could not understand how Alice's brother could come in the room and catch a man with his naked sister…and not be *enraged*.

Alice smiled at her brother and said, "It's looking like I will not find a husband now at my age, so when we get back, I will start to do your work. The extra money you bring home will come in handy." She said, giving her brother a kiss on the cheek.

With that, John said, "Don't be long, Freddie – I want to learn more about these engines…" and left the two of them together in the bathroom.

"Are you okay with me being here?" asked Freddie.

"Why do you ask?" said Alice.

"You have no clothes on...and....I can see you..." replied Freddie.

"I don't understand...what different does that make? My clothes would've gotten wet had I left them on..." asked a puzzled Alice.

"I had better leave..." said Freddie.

"You have gone red in the face, Freddie Chambers!" she said. Then she looked into his eyes. "You *like me...don't you*?"

He coughed and put his head down. Alice stopped playing with the bubbles and stood up in the bath. Although dwarfed by Freddie, she managed to place her finger under his chin and raise his head. "Do you want to *kiss me...Freddie?*"

Mr. Chambers was now sporting a crimson face as he hesitatingly nodded his head. Alice stood on her tippy-toes and Freddie bent down. As their lips met, they both enjoyed a sensation that was brand new. It was the *one thing Alice had always wanted...and the one thing Freddie had never really thought about...until now.* This was DEFINITELY a case of *love at first kiss*. As the breathtaking smooch came to an end, Freddie was first to speak.

"What are we doing? When the storm comes back...and it *will* come back...all this will *be over...and we will never see each other again*!"

"I know...but for me, this short time with you will last a *lifetime...*" said Alice.

"Same here." He replied, as he once again pressed his eager lips upon Alice's soft mouth. Her eyes closed, as she felt the depth of his kiss. Her body went limp as the feeling of *euphoria* bloomed in every part of her body. Freddie was feeling the same tingle as his arms came to rest around her upper body. This lover's clinch seemed to enhance their mutual lust, as they both felt one another's body in this way for the very first time. Freddie looked into Alice's eyes as she stared into his. He smiled sweetly at her and wrapped a towel around her shoulders, and began to dry her.

The thought of what he could do right now filled his mind…but the gentleman in him resisted the temptation.

"We have only *one week* to last us *the rest of our days*…so let's make it a *week to remember…*" Freddie said.

"And what a week it will be…" said Alice, "What wonderful things we can do together!" she continued.

Freddie nodded his head and said, "It will be a *glorious week* for us both…"

This time there was a knock on the door, followed by John popping his head round the corner. "Sis! Please, put some clothes on or Freddie will *never* come in here and read to me about these engines!"

This time it was Freddie and Alice's turn to look at each other and burst into laughter.

"We have plans to make, my beautiful Alice…" said Freddie.

"I know, and *I can't wait!*" said Alice, as she threw her arms around him once more.

"We will be right in, John." Freddie said.

With a broad smile on his face, John retreated back to the living room and his books. Alice stepped back from Freddie. She undid the towel that Freddie had placed around her and it fell to the ground. She then stepped back towards Freddie, and he lifted her off the ground as he gave her the biggest smile and squeeze she had ever had in her entire life.

"Will you promise to love me?" she asked.

"I already do, my sweet little Alice…" he said with a smile.

A Switch in Time

Alice's face beamed as tears of joy welled up in her eyes and caressed her cheeks and she said, "Nobody has ever loved me...in that way. The boys in my time never wanted to have anything to do with me. After awhile, I settled down into thinking that I must be ugly...so I stopped thinking about finding my gentleman for the *longest time*...but now, here you are, holding me, and I am naked and unashamed...and it is the *best feeling in the world.*"

Again, Freddie hugged his newfound love and kissed her ever-so-gently.

After drying herself, Alice went back to the pile of clothes she had taken off and began to redress, but Freddie stopped her and said, "Wait a minute, Alice...I shall get you a dressing gown so that you will be more comfortable." He left the bathroom and made his way into the bedroom, where he found one of Alicia's satin dressing gowns. To his surprise as he came out of the bedroom, there was Alice, standing with her brother looking over his shoulder at the pictures of steam engines. She was *still naked*, and Freddie thought to himself how wonderful it would be to be as unworried as one's body as these people from history were.

As Freddie placed the gown around Alice, he sat at John's side and said to him, "Would you like to go see one of those tomorrow?"

John leapt up from his seat and said, "I would *love it!* But I thought you said we couldn't go out..."

"Yes...I did say that...but I've decided that I am *not the keeper of time*, and my job is merely to protect you both. The thing is...it has gone *beyond* that now, because I have fallen in love with your sister...and I don't think that was part of the deal. So *what the hell*...let's go and *have some FUN.*"

"You two have *fallen in love*? How is that going to work? We have to return to our *own time*, Alice..." said a worried John.

"It's okay, John – you have nothing to worry about. This love affair will only last as long as I am here…but in reality, it will last me *the rest of my life*. And like I said earlier, it will stop me from trying to find a husband, and I will be free to do *your work* while you better yourself." Said a very mature-sounding Alice.

"Then I am happy for the both of you – and I will give you as much free time as it is possible to give, so you can enjoy what time you have together." Said John.

The three friends all sat down, and Freddie began to read to John. John was the most captivated audience Freddie had ever had – he was listening to *every detail* of what Freddie read.

"I've never heard anyone read before…" said Alice. "It's so beautiful!"

Freddie gave her a little smile and continued reading about how the pressured steam was forced into the pistons, which then moved the push-rods, which then turned the wheels, making the engine move forward…and John was *lapping it up*.

After a couple of hours, John said, "I'm tired now, and it sounds like we are going to have a big day tomorrow, so why don't I sleep in here on this wonderful long seat…and you two go in there?" He pointed at the bedroom.

"Are you *sure* you don't mind, John?" Freddie asked, taking hold of Alice's hand.

"You say a *week*…but we don't really *know* how long we're going to be here…so I don't think we have any time to waste. If you two are going to live a life in this short period of time, I don't think you should be hanging around!" John said with a smile.

"I *love you*, John…" Alice said, giving her brother a kiss on his forehead.

"Cheers, brother." Freddie added.

The loving couple exited the living room and entered the bedroom, where the king-sized bed awaited. As they began to

A Switch in Time

undress, Freddie was thinking of Alice's honour, and said, "Tonight, we will sleep together but we will not make love. I have a friend who can marry us tomorrow…it will not be a Christian wedding in a church…but it will be just as binding. It is called a *handfasting*. So if that is okay with you, then we shall make love."

"So I will be a *married lady*?" asked Alice with a smile.

"You most *certainly will*, my dear." Replied Freddie.

The two lovers embraced, and the last thing they saw before they drifted into slumber was each-other's eyes closing.

John stood on the balcony looking out into the night, thinking about his sister finally finding love…and what tomorrow might bring for his sister, himself…and the rest of their lives.

The following day arrived; it was still dark when John opened his eyes. He quickly left the sofa and made his way to the bedroom door. Once inside, he jumped on the bed and shouted, "Come on, you two, it's time to get up!"

Alice and Freddie woke with a start.

"What do you want John…it's *very* early…moaned Freddie."

"It's time to get up and *go!* It's almost 6:30!" said an excited John.

"There is nowhere open, John…not until 9 o'clock! Go back to sleep for an hour or two…" suggested a yawning Freddie.

"I can't go back to sleep – I'm too excited!" was John's quick reply.

Freddie looked at Alice and said, "C'mon Alice…I doubt that John will go back to sleep, so we might as well get up…"

Knowing her brother, Alice quickly agreed and threw back the bedcovers. Freddie was reminded once again of his soon-to-be-wife's beauty.

"*Good morning, darling...*" he whispered adoringly.

"Good morning, Freddie!" she said with a grin.

The betrothed couple kissed and got out of the bed from either side. By now, the excited John was back in the living room. Alice enquired as to what she would wear today. Freddie took her hand and led her to Alicia's walk-in wardrobe. The look of *amazement* on Alice's face was a sight to see as she surveyed Alicia's vast collection.

"You can wear anything you like, Alice...You will find it will all probably fit you." Instructed Freddie.

"*Anything??*" she answered excitedly.

"Anything your little heart desires, my love..." he answered.

Whilst Freddie put his clothes back on, Alice ran up and down the corridor of clothing that belonged to Alicia. Finally deciding on a blouse and long skirt, Freddie led her into the bathroom, filled the sink with water, and let her wash herself. Not wanting to get into explaining the brushing of teeth, he decided a wash would suffice and brought her back into the bedroom.

"The underwear drawer is probably one of those in the dressing table..." said Freddie.

"*Underwear? What is...underwear...Freddie?*"

Freddie looked embarrassed, and with a slight cough answered, "You know...*knickers and stuff...*"

"What are *knickers*?" she asked.

"Ohh dear...erm...do you not wear them in your time?" he asked nervously.

Alice just shook her head, shrugged her shoulders and said, "No."

"I will show you." He said as he moved over to the dressing table.

He began opening the drawers until he came to the one that housed Alicia's underwear. Every single item in the drawer was *new and still in its packet*, as Alicia never wore the same pair of underwear twice. Freddie took a pair out of its packet and held them in front of Alice. He then pointed to where they went. When she saw them, she remembered taking something like that off the previous night before she got in the bath. Freddie bent down and opened the top of them so she could place her feet into each hole, and then slid them up her unshaven legs.

"What are these for?" asked Alice.

Once again, Freddie struggled to find the right words. "Ahem...they are for..." Freddie paused struggling to find the right words. "I don't really *know* their practical use. Both men and women wear them in these times."

"*Men wear things like this?*" asked Alice, with a giggle in her voice.

"No...uhh...not *exactly* like those...men's underwear is slightly different. Anyway, they look great on you! Just put the skirt and the blouse on, and you will be ready." He said, not wanting to enter the mine field of explaining what a *bra* was.

The next hour was spent in the bathroom. This time, Alice was the teacher as she took her brother's hand and led him in. She filled the bathtub just as Freddie had done the previous night, then turned to her brother and said, "Take off your clothes and get in."

John immediately stripped off his clothes and entered the tub. Alice took hold of the sponge and began to wash her brother's back.

"Are you *sure* you're ok with what is going on?" she asked.

"Yes. I've always liked it when you wash my back...you're much gentler than our mother..." said John with a smile.

"You *know* I don't mean that!" said Alice, slapping him over the head with the sponge.

John burst into laughter as the bubbles rushed over his head. He turned and looked at his sister. "Of course I'm *okay with it...it means you will find the love you have ALWAYS WANTED. I am so pleased for you! I know you thought it would NEVER HAPPEN. And we do know that strange things happen for a REASON. Maybe you finding love is WHY WE ARE HERE, sis...*"

"I think good will come of our adventures...for both you and me...and for Freddie and the two people back in *our time...I REALLY believe that, John...*" she answered.

While the two Victorian siblings were in the bathroom, Freddie was on the phone with his friend Susan, organizing the handfasting he had promised Alice the night before. Susan had quite a busy day arranged, but said she would be able to rearrange her first appointment as long as they could be early. This was perfect for Freddie, as he was already up at an ungodly hour for him.

As soon as his bath was over, John was keen to get out. He was feeling happier to have a chaperone from this era, in case any more *dragons* showed up.

"Okay guys – let's get our coats and head out into town!"

The two siblings were in their winter coats faster than Freddie could get the words out. The door to the elevator slid open with its usual *whoosh*. Freddie stepped inside. John and Alice remained outside, looking very apprehensive.

"Come on in, you two...it's not going to hurt you..." Freddie reassured them.

The two very uncertain siblings gingerly stepped inside the elevator. Alice quickly took hold of Freddie's hand, and to his surprise, so did *John.* He had already depressed the 'ground' button, and the elevator effortlessly began to move downwards. The Victorian couple let out simultaneous whimpers as the first elevator trip of their lives began. As soon as the doors reopened,

A Switch in Time

John and Alice ran out into the safety of the lobby. Freddie strolled out shaking his head, but with a wry smile on his face. Through another door and out into the big, wide world strolled these three friends.

"The first thing we will do is visit my friend Susan Leybourne." Said Freddie. "I have already been in touch with her, and she has agreed to perform the ceremony!" he excitedly continued.

"What ceremony?" enquired John.

"We are to be *married*, brother..." said Alice with a smile on her face the likes of which John had never seen.

"Well that sounds a *grand start to the day!*" replied John.

Freddie just smiled, and arm-in-arm with Alice, they began the relatively short stroll to a wooded area just outside of town.

Upon arriving at the rendezvous point, Freddie was pleased to see his friend Susan already there and waiting. Susan shook both John and Alice's hands and greeted them both. She said to John, "You will be the one to bear witness to this union."

She turned to Freddie and Alice, and asked, "Is the binding you require for *this life...or for all lives to come...*"

The soon to be wed couple looked at each other and mouthed the words *All Lives* to each other. They simultaneously nodded, then turned to Susan and said together, "*All lives.*"

Susan smiled, as that was the answer she had wanted to hear.

Although it was cold, it was a wonderfully sunny day, and the bare trees of winter looked magnificent against the backdrop of a deep blue cloudless sky. Susan began the ceremony, and after a short time, she was physically tying the couple's hands together with the cord she had made especially for them after the call she had received from Freddie. The ceremony lasted around twenty minutes, with thanks being given to each other, and the old Pagan Gods. At the end of the ceremony, with their hands still tied, Susan led them to the broomstick that was lying on the ground. She invited them to jump over it to seal their union. Freddie and Alice jumped the broom and brought the ceremony to a wonderful conclusion. Freddie asked Susan if she would care to join them for their wedding breakfast. Susan, however, had to decline the request due to the other appointments she had already booked. She bade John and Alice goodbye, kissed Freddie on the cheek and whispered in his ear, "*I want the whole story next week...*"

With that, she smiled once again at all three of them, bid them farewell and turned and walked away. Freddie picked Alice up in his arms and kissed her passionately. John said, "Wedding breakfast?"

Freddie smiled and said, "I hope you're hungry!"

"I am indeed!" said John.

"Me too!" said Alice.

"Well then, little wife and brother – follow me..." said Freddie as they made their way to his favourite café in the centre of Leeds. There, they all three enjoyed a full English breakfast with tea and extra toast. The two Victorians loved every mouthful, as did Freddie...but he spent more time looking at his new wife than he did eating his breakfast. The rest of the day was spent exploring Leeds...looking at the shops, watching the street artists, and generally having a *good time*. Freddie didn't mind being chaperoned by John, because there was nothing he was able to do about it. There wasn't an out-of-time Victorian crèche to leave him at, and he knew that John was in his care, just as much as Alice was.

A Switch in Time

CHAPTER EIGHT

The afternoon was bright, as all the boat crew, including Jamie and young James was hard at work cleaning and fixing Albert's pride and joy. Working alongside his sister was something Jamie had never done...nor wanted to do...yet now, he was seeing his sister in a different light. Although he was expecting her to blow up at any time, because he couldn't get the old Alicia out of his mind, this was now the SECOND day, and the Victorian era that Jamie loved was indeed changing his *sister*. Unlike him, it wasn't the majesty, ingenuity and industry of the period that was changing her, it was the *poverty,* the *poor* and the *undernourished* that were working on Alicia. Jamie had skipped over this part of the Victorian era, as he was only *really* interested in the Industrial part. It was an eye-opener for Jamie just as much as it was for Alicia. By now, the side of the barge that Alicia had been cleaning was sparkling and all finished. Albert strolled over to where she was and put his arm around her shoulder.

"Well done, Alicia! You have done a very good job of work! You should be proud of yourself – because I'm proud of you! He said to her smiling.

"I *am* proud...but it took me a lot longer than it took Doris."

"Yes...it *did*...but Doris has been doing this for a *very long time* – and she has her own way of getting it done...if Doris was in *your time*, *you* would be doing things faster than *her*." Comforted Albert.

"No I wouldn't...she would *still be faster than me in my time as well*...I'm hoping that will change, though..." answered Alice.

"You are *already making that change*, sis..." said Jamie.

"I hope so, brother...because I'm beginning to *hate who I am*." She answered.

"Who you *were*..." replied Jamie.

"Where has that little bugger gone off to now?" said Doris with her hands on her hips, looking at the empty spot where the horse and idle child should be.

"I shall go find him – I saw the direction he headed off in..." laughed Alicia.

Alicia, still dirty from her toils, climbed down from the barge and onto the towpath and said, "It won't take me long – we will be back soon."

"Make sure you clip him around the ear when you find him!" instructed Doris.

"Let's have that kettle on, Doris, while I find out what young Jamie did this morning!" said Albert.

Doris went below deck and made a cup of tea whilst Albert and Jamie began speaking about what Jamie's job entailed.

Jamie explained to Albert it was an *engineering factory powered by STEAM...and they actually made STEAM LOCOMOTIVES!* He went on to tell Albert that he had secured an apprenticeship to the engineer...a position much sought-after in this day and age. Albert explained to Jamie that it was also his son John's wish to have such a job, and how much he would *love* to do it.

"The position will be *his* when I go back to my time and he returns here." Said Jamie.

"How will that work? Your boss will be expecting *you* next week...what will happen when my John turns up?" puzzled Albert.

"Haven't you *noticed*, Albert...none of the people you have around here have asked who we are, or to the whereabouts of John and Alice?" asked Jamie.

"I reckon that's because while this has been happening, you two must look like my two..." answered Albert.

"That's *exactly right*! I have registered myself at the factory as *John Watson*!" said Jamie.

"John is not as clever as you...people there will *notice*..." said Albert.

"No they won't notice! Because by next week, it is all down to being *taught by the engineer*...to him, learning the trade hands-on is *better than having a University degree*...so all John will need is *enthusiasm and an ability to WORK HARD*."

"There is no doubting my boy's enthusiasm and willingness to work!" smiled Albert.

"I will write everything down that I am doing just as I do it, so that he can study all that I will have done this week. Do you know anybody that can read?" Jamie enquired.

"I can't read myself, but my friend Bert Wheelwright can!" said Albert.

"Then *he* can *read my instructions to John!*" Jamie answered excitedly.

"Who will help me on the barge?" asked Albert.

"I'm not sure – but if this is how things are supposed to work out, it will be sorted." Comforted John.

Alicia was about a quarter of a mile down the towpath when she spotted Toby and James. As soon as she reached them, James covered his ears with both hands.

"I'm not going to smack you…" she said with a smile.

James removed his hands from his ears. Toby just twitched his.

"Do you ride Toby? She asked him.

"No." replied James, wiping his nose on his sleeve and putting his flat cap back on. "*You're not my sister.*" He continued.

"You know then? She answered, surprised. "No – I'm not your sister…but your sister will be back very soon."

"I don't mind you…you're soft and you don't clout me round the ear…" he said.

Alicia smiled and held her hand out towards little James. She was pleased she was standing on the side of him of the sleeve that didn't receive the handkerchief treatment. As the tiny boy's hand grasped tightly onto hers, she said, "C'mon James – it's almost teatime, I'll bet you're hungry!"

James nodded his head and with one hand in Alicia's and the other on Toby's harness, they made their way back to the barge. On the way back they past a large building on the side of the canal. Alicia noticed small children peering out of the large barred, broken windows.

"What's this place?" she asked with some trepidation.

"That's the *work house.* And if I don't pull my socks up, it's where I'm going…" he said.

"What do you mean?" enquired Alicia.

"Whenever I do anything wrong, my mum always says, '*If you don't pull your socks up, lad, it's the work house for you!*'" he answered.

"Ohhh…I see…" she answered with a little giggle.

Then Alicia caught a glimpse of one of the poor creatures staring at them. She *knew* they were looking at the two of them with *envious eyes*. The different levels of *poorness* were hard for her to understand …*poor people were a 'waste of space' and should be 'kept in their place'* was was her mother had taught her…and here she was, looking at that very thing. Those words now weighed *very heavily in her heart*. She grasped even tighter onto James' hand as they left the depressing scene. Before long Alicia, young James and Toby were back at the barge.

"It's alright Doris – when I found him he was grooming Toby." Informed Alicia.

Doris gave James one of her looks that said *'I'm watching you, lad'*. He knew this look all to well, and scurried downstairs to where a jam sandwich was awaiting his arrival.

"We past a work house on the way back…it was *awful*. There were children staring at us from the windows…it was *pitiful*. They seemed to be staring at *James*…" Alicia said.

"They envy his *easy life*." Said Doris.

"They think James' life is *easy?"* answered Alicia in disbelief.

"At the side of what those poor urchins have to do, James has a *charmed life*." Instructed Doris.

Alicia *knew* what a charmed life was…and getting up at daybreak and tending a horse for up to *twelve hours*, depending upon the time of year, in her opinion wasn't charmed at all. This made her think what it must be like inside one of these buildings…and *most of all how those poor children must be suffering*. Suddenly she realized that she had been thinking of that word 'poor', again…it was *different* this time, because it wasn't a derogatory word…she was beginning to realize there were more than two types of people in this world. To the 2013 Alicia, there were only *rich* people and *poor* people…but the Victorian version of Alicia was realizing it *wasn't about money at all*. In fact, the realization was that poor people's family lives and their working lives were *just as*

A Switch in Time

important to them as rich people's lives...and this time she understood WHY.

The stove was burning brightly, and sat in a semi-circle around it were Albert, Doris, Alicia, Jamie and young James – all of whom felt totally satisfied after their tea of jam and bread.

"A good day's work from everyone today!" announced Albert as he lit his pipe. "We will carry on cleaning, painting and mending the barge while you are at work tomorrow, Jamie, and then the barge will be finished. I will do the short run to Thwaite Gate and back, so you will be able to find us along the towpath after work." He continued.

"That sounds good to me!" said Jamie.

"Did you say *painting*, Albert?" asked Alicia.

"Yes I did...do you have a steady hand, Alicia?" he enquired.

"No-one can paint fingernails like me!" said Alicia.

"That's true, Albert...she has had *a lot of practise sitting around fingernail-painting*!" laughed Jamie.

Alicia just stuck her tongue out at him. Everybody laughed, and Jamie suddenly realized he was in a *family environment with his sister...and LOVING IT!*

"Why do you paint your fingernails?" asked Doris.

"It's just one of the things women do in my time..." answered Alicia.

"You can't get much work done if you are sitting around painting your nails!" observed Doris.

This banter carried on until it was time for bed. It was *strange* how Alicia didn't seem to mind the smell that had caused her *so much trouble* the previous night...nor did the sleeping arrangements bother her. The family of boat people all settled down together in their little cabin, and as the fire died down, the heat of their bodies kept them warm all through the night, until it was time for Doris to rise and restart the stove.

The next day, Alicia woke to droplets of water dripping down on her face.

"We have a leak!" she shouted, to alert everyone to the danger.

"You don't need to worry about a leak from above, lass...it's the ones *underneath* that you need to lose sleep over." Answered Albert reassuringly.

"It's just *condensation*, Alicia..." Jamie added.

Although Alicia was changing her ways, she would still have preferred it to be *rain* rather than *other people's sweat*...but unlike the other Alicia, who would've screamed and run to the shower, she just turned over so her head wasn't under the drip anymore, and fell back to sleep. The next thing she knew Doris was gently shaking her arm to wake her up.

"C'mon lass, we have a lot to do. I will go get some kindling while you get your boots on, and we will make a fire."

"No, Doris...just give me a minute to get my boots and coat on and I will get it." Said Alicia.

Doris had a little tear in her eye.

"Whatever is the matter, Doris?" enquired Alicia.

"Oh...I'm just being silly..." replied Doris.

"No...please tell me..." urged Alicia.

"It was just for a second when I woke you up – you smiled at me and I thought my Alice was back...now you have begun to smile you look like her..." said Doris.

Amongst all other things Alicia was feeling...firstly the horror for herself from being in that filthy, disgusting time period...then when she saw the *abject poverty* of the children in the work houses and the conditions people lived in...she had not spared a

A Switch in Time

thought for the fact that Albert and Doris' children had been *taken away from them*. Alicia put her arms around Doris and gave her a loving squeeze.

"Your Alice will be back with you soon, Doris, and things will return to normal."

"I know..." Doris answered. "Now, let's get that wood and light a fire..." she continued.

Alicia put her coat on and slid the hatch open, which released the two doors, and she was out in the morning air.

Unlike the day before, the sky was unclear and it was snowing. The snow was unlike any she had seen before – this was because it had come through the soot from the tall chimneys, and was tinged with black. Not wanting to stay too long in the cold, she hurried to find as much kindling as she could hold, then headed back towards the barge. It was when she was on her way back that she saw a horrific sight.

Two children...a little boy and girl...were sitting under a bush. With nothing covering them when the weathered turned freezing cold, it had frozen them where they sat. Alicia dropped her wood and tried to get ahold of one of them by the arm...but the little girl was stiff, and lifeless. Her blue lips were set in a fatal frown. Frozen tears lined her white cheeks, and her pale blue eyes had lost their sparkle, staring ahead into nothingness, but boring into her very soul. The little boy's last facial expression embedded itself into Alicia's mind like a burning hot branding iron. This tiny boy had the look of a lost soul...hoping for a saviour that had never come. Both children were barefoot, and their little toes were black with frostbight. Their ragged clothes, which barely covered them, were threadbare – no protection at all from the bitter cold. Alicia screamed out to Doris for help. When she arrived, she said to Alicia, "C'mon lass...this is a *common sight for this time of year…believe me…they are better off where they are now."*

"*A common sight??! My GOD! What will happen to them?"* cried Alicia.

"The *undertaker* walks along the canal path *every morning* in winter with his handcart along this path. He will pick them up…and all the *other* unfortunate ones who didn't make it through the night…" informed the hardened Doris.

"Do you mean…there will be *more of them?"* asked Alicia in horror, her mouth gaping.

"Yes. I'm afraid they are caught out when the weather turns…as it did last night." Doris replied.

"I can't believe it! They are just *little children!* They should be *at home with their parents! Children shouldn't be LEFT OUT IN THE COLD TO DIE!"* said Alicia with tears streaming down her cheeks.

"Try not to upset yourself, Alicia. These poor little ones don't *have parents*…they have run away from the horrible work houses. This is what I meant when I said they are *better off."* Informed Doris with a grim look on her face.

Alicia picked up the sticks that she had dropped and put them under her arm. She took hold of Doris' hand, and the two sad ladies made their way back to the barge to light the fire.

Upon arriving back, Albert and Jamie were awake, and already breaking the icy away from the boat. Jamie saw his sister's tear-stained face and asked, "What's wrong, Alicia?"

Alicia just shook her head…but Doris answered for her.

"She has just had a shock, that's all…she will be fine soon."

The two women went below deck.

"Like as not, they will have come across some dead young'uns." Said Albert.

"Do you mean...*dead...children??*" asked Jamie in horror.

"I do indeed, young lad. We live in hard times – and homeless children can be the ones who have it *hardest* – especially at this time of year."

"I'd better go see to Alicia...it will have disturbed her terribly!" worried Jamie.

"Leave her be lad! These are the things *she is meant to see*. These are the things that *make her think about her life*. It's not *comfort* she needs, it's a dose of *reality*...and there is no better place to find that than here." Instructed Albert.

Jamie nodded his head and said, "You are right, Albert. I was forgetting why we are here. There is one thing I have found out about my sister, and that is, she *does have a good side*...and I am seeing her *quite differently than I ever have before.*"

"One thing I've noticed lad, is that now we are seeing her smile, she has the look of *my Alice...*" answered Albert in an agreeing tone.

The two men continued their ice-breaking around the boat.

Below deck, Doris had lit the fire and Alicia had filled the kettle. Soon, breakfast was underway. Doris took a clean cloth and dipped it into a bowl of water. Wringing the surplus water out, she cleaned Alicia's tear-stained face.

"I don't know *why* you have to *see such sadness*...a pretty girl like you should spend her time being *happy* and *loved by her family*. I would love you if you were my daughter, as I love our Alice. In this life, we have to be happy with what we have...otherwise, *we have nothing*. In a way, Albert and I are very *rich*...believe me, you don't need lots of money to have happiness! I would not change my life for anything!" said Doris.

"I have been such a *bitch*. Just before we came here, I made a young man who was *extremely good as what he did* JOBLESS. I cared not of what anguish this would cause him! I just *enjoyed the power of being able to do it.* I *knew what he was saying was true...but I still demanded what I WANTED.* I am seeing a link between that and those poor, unfortunate children...I'm not saying he will suffer the same fate...I'm just seeing a *link.*"

"Well then – I'm not saying that I understand what is going on, but it seems to me you are *changing for the better.* When you get

back, you can put what you have learned here to some good use!" said Doris.

"Don't you worry about that, Doris! I will leave the *old Alicia here*...and I will try to put to right my wrongs. I feel it will take me some time...because I have wronged *many people*...and now, for the first time, my heart feels *heavy.* One of my favourite stories from childhood was a novel by Charles Dickens, called *'A Christmas Carol'*...it was a story about an old miser who changed into a good person...I hope it works in real life..."

How ponderous is my chain? Thought Alicia.

The two women made breakfast and called the men down to eat. Breakfast was once again tea and toast. They sat down and began their simple meal.

"What are you doing today, Alicia?" Jamie asked.

Before she had time to answer, Albert said, "She's *steering the boat to Thwaite Gate and back!"*

"Am I?" said a surprised Alicia.

"You are indeed!" Albert replied.

Alicia's face beamed with excitement. "It will be like steering the yacht!"

Jamie shook his head and said, "I don't quite think so..." But, he was amused by his sister being told to work and her excitement over it.

"Well – it's time for me to go to work!" announced Jamie.

"Wait! I made you some sandwiches!" said Alicia.

Yet more surprises from his ever-changing sister! He thought.

By now, young James had woken up, had had his breakfast, and was already outside tending to Toby's needs. Once he had been harnessed, James took him over the bridge to the opposite bank of the canal. Albert moved to the bow of the barge and started to pole the boat to the other side. The ice was cracking as Albert's large forearms powered down upon the pole. It wasn't long before the barge was facing the opposite direction, towards Thwaite Gate – and his next load of coal from Middleton Pit. When the rope had been tied to Toby's harness, James made a clicking noise and led Toby by a rope. He wasn't tall enough yet to hold Toby's harness. The strong rope slowly began to tighten as the slack was taken up. It lifted from the icy-cold water and snapped taught with a spray of water droplets exploding into the air, and the coal barge began to move.

Albert had now joined Alicia at the stern, and explained to her that the bow would want to move towards the canal bank, with it being pulled from there.

"Just push the tiller arm a little towards the bank, and that will rectify the horse's pull...then you will be steering nice and straight." He advised.

"This is fun!" exclaimed Alicia, not even thinking of the cold biting at her face.

James and Toby pulled the barge, steered by Alicia and crewed by Albert and Doris, down the towpath and out of the city centre, making their way to Thwaite Gate. Jamie was walking in the opposite direction towards Holbeck. He arrived at his new place of work fifteen minutes early. He went to the engine house to look at the steam engine. As he walked inside...there it was...*a real steam engine at work, powering a FACTORY.* He had only seen one in a museum...but this was one in its *golden years*, as the new technology! A man was sitting in an arm chair. He was the chap who was looking after the engine! He introduced himself to Jamie as Alf Chandler.

"Hello!" said Jamie. "I'm the new apprentice to the engineer! I just wanted to come and have a look at this *magnificent engine of yours!*" he explained.

"Hello to *you*, young fellow! So, you like *steam engines,* do ya? Mine's a *beauty!* They are a *living, breathing thing, you know...*" Alf informed him.

"I totally agree! The one I am restoring at the moment shall one day *burst into life*...they are not just pieces of metal, like some people think!" he enthused.

"*Restored?"* mused Alf Chandler.

Realizing his mistake again, Jamie began to think that this was going to be harder than he originally thought.

"I've used the wrong word again, haven't I? I do that trying to make myself look like I know what I am saying...*but I keep using the wrong words*...sorry about that...I meant to say...*re-boring*...which is what I will be doing today with the engineer..." cringed the embarrassed new apprentice.

"Sounds a tricky job! I'm looking at the clock on my wall...I think you'd better make your way inside, lad!" said Mr. Chandler, lacing his fingers under his flat cap and scratching his head.

Jamie bid him good day and left the room, knowing he had better stop thinking about this time period in past tense!

Quick smart, he made his way to the factory, where the work force were approaching their machinery, and to the belt drives, to slide the power belts onto the fly wheels of their individual machines. The instant noise was *deafening* to Jamie...but to the people around him, they just carried on as if the decibel level hadn't even altered.

"Good morning, John!" came a booming voice from the office. "Let's have you in 'ere!" said Jack Hawkins. "As I said yesterday,

A Switch in Time

I want you to learn hands ON. Your history degree won't help you here – what we are doing is *too modern* – you will have to use your *common sense*...and another thing...if the young lads working in here find out you are a bit of a toff, you will have a *big problem with them.*"

"So...if I forget what I've learned at University and pretend I'm from a poor background...the people here will *like me more?"* he asked. "What about *you?"* he continued, looking straight into Jack Hawkins' eyes.

"Me, lad? I never had *time* for schooling...I was taught how to *read and write by my uncle*...but then I made my own way in life. I don't really hold with *fancy universities*...my belief is that *skills are learned in a FACTORY, not a CLASSROOM..."* was his truthful answer.

"I've never *been* to University..." said Jamie.

"What!" replied the Works Manager.

"I said that to *impress you*...I can't read...or write. I only know about these engines because a *friend* taught me a bit about them. I'm a canal boatman...like my father before me. But I *so desperately want to be an engineer! I want to be PART of this MODERN ERA!*" announced Jamie.

Jack Hawkins sat down at his desk. He looked once again at the drawings lying there. He then looked up at Jamie, raising a single eyebrow, and asked, "Why the deceit?"

"I didn't want to leave my father's business to work as a *boiler man*...I want to *be an engineer!* If I had told you the *truth*...you would never had gotten to see my potential! I need you to *know* that I *understand* about what you are building here! If you can forgive the pretense...I will make the *best apprentice you have ever had.*" Replied Jamie.

Jack Hawkins wore a more relaxed facial expression and said, "Although I *don't condone lying in ANY SHAPE OR FORM*, you have owned up to your deceit...and your argument is a JUST

John Paul Bernett

ONE. You may well become the *best apprentice I've ever had...but do not deceive me ever again...and you will gain my TRUST, along with my KNOWLEDGE.* Now – do you remember that I said I would have preferred you to start next week? That is because I have to leave for four days...I will be out of town...so your training will start at the beginning of *next week*. So for now, you can just familiarize yourself with the factory."

The Works Manager packed his bag with papers and drawings. He placed his top hat on his head and made for the door. The two men shook hands, with Jamie marvelling at his luck. *John would be able to walk RIGHT IN...and be HIMSELF.*

*This must be fate...*thought Jamie...for he now had the run of the factory, and no need to write down instructions that John wouldn't be able to read anyway.

A Switch in Time

CHAPTER 9

As Freddie, John and Alice left the café on Vicar Lane, the bright winter sun against the deepest blue sky made all three of them scowl. Freddie reached into his top pocket, pulling out a pair of sunglasses and placing them over his eyes. John and Alice gawked at him.

"What is that you have just put over your eyes?" she asked.

"These are my *sunglasses*...they stop the *harmful rays of the sun from damaging my eyes.*" Explained Freddie.

"You are silly, Freddie! There are no *harmful rays in the sun...the sun is good! My father says, the sun keeps us warm and helps things to grow!* She answered.

"Your father is *absolutely right,* the sun *does do those things...*but in this time, we have damaged the ozone layer, which protects us from the *harmful rays.*" Instructed Freddie.

The two Victorians wore a puzzled expression. Looking at the siblings faces, Freddie knew this would take a lot of explaining, so he simplified it by saying, "In *your time* the protection around the Earth is in good condition – only the warmth and light come through. In this century, our greed for money and power, and the building of super-factories, that spill the *worst kind of pollution*

A Switch in Time

into the air, has taken its toll. Because of this, the sun is slowly *killing us all*." Said Freddie.

John and Alice looked at each other. Turning to Freddie, John asked, "Do these people *know* they are *destroying the Earth?*"

"Umm...*yes...they DO...*" he answered.

"Well tell them to *stop doing it!* And then your time will be safe like ours!" said Alice.

Freddie smiled, as he knew they were RIGHT. In their time, if something broke, it could be *fixed*. This only increased his view that the root of all evil was *money*. The only reasons for the problems of society now were because of a tiny part of the world's population's needs to keep *polluting the planet* to *make money...money they could never spend in MANY LIFETIMES*. Having been taught the simplest lesson that even a small child would have understood, Freddie decided that their had been enough political talk and now was the time *for FUN*. With a tight grip on his wife's hand, all three of them headed for the shops, for Alice...and the museums for John.

"This is a *wonderland!*" announced Alice. "Everything *sparkles! The whole place is magical! It's a dream that I want to stay in FOREVER!!*" she continued.

"Yes...but this is all *frilly girl stuff...*" complained John.

"Your time is coming, John. In fact, I have just had an idea..." said Freddie. "You come with me and John, Alice...I want to take him somewhere..."

"But that's not fair! If we take John to see his engine thingies, we will never get him out, and I will have to spend the *whole day* being bored!" protested Alice, sporting a frown.

"Just because you're the oldest doesn't mean we have to do everything you want!" instructed her older brother.

"Now, now – stop it – the pair of you! I said I had an idea, and here it is: We shall take John to Armley Mills, where he can spend the *entire day* looking at the exhibits...and then, later this afternoon we shall go back and pick him up, and bring him back to the penthouse! That way, you'll get to look around the shops, Alice, and you, John, can fill yourself with all the Victorian engineering your head can hold!" said Freddie quite triumphantly.

"You are *such a clever man*, my Freddie!" Alice said.

"Yes, you *are*!" agreed John.

Freddie just stood there enjoying his moment of diplomacy, feeling quite pleased with himself. The thing now was...he had to get his two wards, who were frightened to enter an elevator, into a *taxi*. John and Alice had already seen cars thundering up and down Vicar Lane – but as yet, were too frightened to enquire as to *what they were*...they were *about to find out*, as all three of them stood in a short line of people queuing at the taxi rank.

John was gazing at the people entering the *strange contraptions*, and asked, in a slightly quivering voice, "What are we *doing*, Freddie?"

"We will have to take a *taxi* to get you to the museum...you must think of it as...our version of a horse-drawn vehicle. You already know, John, about how steam engines can pull coaches. You also know that *those coaches used to be pulled by horses*...you have to accept that the *motor car is the evolution of a horse and carriage...*" informed Freddie.

"If I get in there...I'll keep my eyes *tightly shut*!" said Alice.

"As long as it doesn't go too fast..." said John.

By the time they had arrived at the front of the line, John and Alice were very nervous...but Freddie reassured them that everything would be okay. All three slid into the back seat of the taxi. The taxi driver closed the door on John's side, whilst Freddie pulled his door shut. After closing John's door, the driver re-entered his seat and asked for their destination.

"We are going to *Armley Mills*, please, driver." Said Freddie.

A Switch in Time

The taxi pulled away from its spot outside the market building and into the busy traffic along Vicar Lane. Both John and Alice let out a gasp of surprise as the taxi driver pulled away.

"What's wrong? Have you never been in a taxi before?" asked the driver.

"Yes...er...they have...they just have...*problems with this kind of thing...they are...special needs.*" Said Freddie, trying to think fast.

"Sorry about that, I didn't think." Said the driver.

John was just about to say something when Freddie placed his finger upon his lips and made a *shush* sound, giving John a wink.

The journey across town, although *mundane* for Freddie, was a roller coaster ride of *excitement and fear* for the Victorian pair. The glass buildings...the throng of people rushing *everywhere*...and all the *wonderful colours* that said people were wearing made this journey, although scary, also very enjoyable. Soon, the journey was over, and the old mill that John recognized was looming in front of them in the guise of *Armley Mills Museum*. All three exited the taxi and Freddie paid the five pound fair.

On entering the museum, they were greeted by a personal friend of Freddie's.

"Hello, Freddie! Are you and Jamie needing some more information on that broken-down engine of yours?" enquired Lee Coates, the museum curator.

"It isn't for me this time – I need *this young man* to have a crash course in locomotive engineering! Said Freddie.

Lee Coates instantly smiled and enquired, "How long do I have him?"

"He can come almost every day this week!" answered Freddie.

"*Almost?*" said Lee with a puzzled look on his face.

"We are not quite sure when he is going back to his time." Said Freddie, instantly recognizing the mistake he had just made.

"*Going back to HIS time??*"

"Tynemouth...he is going back to Tynemouth..." came the quick reply from Freddie.

Lee put a friendly arm around John's shoulder and said, "Welcome onboard! Now – since Freddie hasn't introduced us, I am Lee. I am the curator of this *fine building*! And what, my dear fellow, would *your* name be?"

"My name is John...and am I going to be *with you all week?*"

"Yes! You can be a friend of the museum...and you can assist me in the *workshop!*" Lee replied.

Moving across to Alice, Lee took hold of her dainty hand. He bent down and gently kissed it, and asked, "Well, who do we have here?"

Giving a little curtsey, Alice said with a smile, "I am Alice! I am Freddie's *wife!*"

"You're *Freddie's WIFE?*" Looking at Freddie, Lee said, "When did *this* happen? And why wasn't I invited to the wedding? And...Freddie...you *don't even have a girlfriend*!"

"I will explain *everything* at the end of the week...but for now, and *don't ask me why because I don't know*...I need John to learn as *much as you can teach him about steam locomotion!*" answered Freddie.

"I've *sussed you out!* I know what's going on!" said Lee.

Freddie looked shocked and stuttered, "Wh-what do you mean...Lee?"

"You're having the *week off to spend with your bride*, and you're leaving me with your apprentice!" said Lee with a proud smile.

"*You've seen clear through me!*" said a very relieved Freddie.

"Okay, then, John, let's find you a pair of overalls! Freddie and Alice, I'll see you both around six o'clock!" was the curator's announcement.

With that, the four people parted company; two of the went into the museum, the other two wrapped their arms around each other and kissed knowing they were *alone* until six o'clock that evening.

"This is *perfect*...we can spend the *whole day together* while John enjoys himself at the museum! In his own way, he will have as good a time as we will! So just for now, let's put John out of our minds and have a good time together. Where would you like to go first, Alice?"

"I would like to go *back to the palace with you...*" she said with a shy grin.

Freddie took out his mobile phone and informed the taxi company that they were ready to leave Armley Mill.

The taxi took no time at all in arriving, and the happy couple made the short ride back to The Calls on the riverside. Upon arriving at the apartment building, they entered the elevator, which delivered them to the penthouse. Once inside, they removed their winter coats, and Alice said, "What do we do now...*husband?*"

"Well..." said Freddie, taking Alice into his arms and walking towards the bedroom. "I think it is time for us to *get to know each other...*" he continued.

"Yes! Yes! YES!" Alice nodded emphatically.

As Freddie made his way to the bedroom, looking into the eyes of this *beautiful maiden from another time*, he began to think how *lucky he was to have her*...but he felt somewhat cheated, for this was the *girl of his dreams*...and soon...she would return to *them*...

"A penny for them?" asked Alice, looking into Freddie's eyes.

"I will have such a short time...how will I *live*...when you go?" said Freddie.

"You will *have me forever...as I will you...*your friend Susan said we will be together for *all our lives...*which means, I will find you *again and again so we will be together FOR ALWAYS.*" She answered.

Her answer made him smile, as he placed his wife gently upon the bed.

"Yes...that is true, my love. Now...have you ever tasted champagne, Alice?" he enquired.

"I don't know – what is it?" she asked.

"It's a sparkling wine with lots of *bubbles!*" said Freddie.

"I have had a drink of elderberry wine once...but it made me go all squiffy..." she replied.

"I think you will be okay with a small glass." Said Freddie, pouring the champagne into two elegant crystal glasses.

Freddie gave a toast. "To Alice and Freddie! This week and FOREVERMORE!"

The two young lovers' glasses touched, making a pretty noise. Alice giggled as the bubbles inevitably went up her nose. This made Freddie smile, as he discovered more and more beautiful things about his beloved *Alice*. Freddie began to undress, but Alice stopped him, saying, "No...let me do that..."

She slipped off his jacket and let it fall to the ground. She smiled as she undid his shirt buttons one by one, revealing Freddie's pale chest. Alice kissed his chest as she unfastened his belt. Freddie felt the waistband of his trousers slacken as Alice undid them. They slipped down his legs and he stepped out of them. Alice took both hands and grasped both legs of his shorts, gently pulling them down over his excited manhood. Alice gasped in shock at the sight of it. This was the first erection she had ever seen. She gazed upon it and couldn't tear her eyes away, wondering what pleasures it might give…and a burning tingle tore its way through her now-moist womanhood. Although both Alice and Freddie had seen each-other naked the previous night…this was *different*. The butterflies in Alice's stomach were dancing like mad and the hair on the back of her neck stood up. All she wanted now was the *magic that happens when two lovers wed.*

Standing naked in front of his wife, Freddie began to disrobe her. First her blouse…with the delicacy of a fine artist, Freddie began to unbutton…as each button gently came undone, he could see under the silky material that she was aroused. He was pleased by this sight, as he had never undressed a woman before in his life and was very nervous. After all the buttons had undone her blouse came apart. There was now a one-inch gap down the centre of her blouse, revealing an ample cleavage. Unlike most women of her century at her age, Alice's breasts were firm and round…most women of her age had had several babies by then…but not Alice…she was still a virgin. Ever so softly, he took hold of her blouse with trembling hands and eased it apart, slipping it over her shoulders and letting it fall to the ground. His heart began to race – seeing Alice for the first time with her beautiful erect nipples. She saw his amazement and said, "I don't really understand this…I'm not *cold*…" said Alice.

"I'm not really up on this sort of thing myself…but I think that happens when you get excited?" John answered. "Shall I continue?"

Alice nodded her head, her eyes wide with anticipation. He undid the buttons of her skirt. She winced as she felt her skirt slide down her legs, joining the rest of her clothes lying on th

e floor. Freddie slid his thumbs under both sides of her underwear and gently slid them down. She stepped away from them shyly, her cheeks tinged with pink. For the first time in both of their lives, this unworldly pair were about to take the first tentative steps of *physical love*. After kissing and holding each-other tight, Freddie picked up his first love and took her to the bed, where they both lay down and began the beautiful process of losing what they had both kept for many years. Alice closed her eyes, and Freddie hoped that all his reading on the subject would help him pleasure his virgin bride.

Over the next hour this inexperienced love-nest was the *happiest place in the world* – and Alice and Freddie were so *deeply in love*. Alice looked deep into Freddie's eyes…so deep, she could almost *see his soul*. As his breath returned to normal he caught her glance…a tearful stare of *love, and wonderment*. He pressed his lips against hers once again, as the now-worldly couple knew what it was to *physically be in love*…and they were in a happy, happy place. The afternoon rolled by in each-other's arms, and any thought of different centuries…or leaving at the end of the week, were gone. As they gently fell into an afternoon doze, they slipped away to the sounds of birds singing, and all was well with the world.

The sound of a door buzzer woke Alice and Freddie from their slumber. It was Lee Coates at the door, delivering John back home. Freddie jumped out of bed and ran to the video bell, depressing the button and seeing Lee standing there.

"We are on the top floor, just come right up!" said Freddie, as he ran back into the bedroom where Alice stood, already dressed.

"It's John, back from the museum!" exclaimed Freddie.

"I'm sure he will tell us all about his day…" laughed Alice."I'm sure he will!" agreed Freddie, as the elevator door whooshed open and the two men walked in.

John ran straight to his sister, exploding with excitement, whilst Lee Coates walked over to Freddie.

"He's had a good day! His interest was *amazing*! He took in everything I taught him! It was as if…this was *brand new technology, and this was his first glimpse of it!* If only I could find more like him, more people would find my museum interesting!" said Lee.

"I'm glad he enjoyed it – I thought he would. He would probably be at the museum *all week if you let him*!" replied Freddie with a laugh.

"In that case, I'll pick him up at 8:30 tomorrow morning, if that's ok with you!" said Lee.

Freddie quickly agreed, then they both turned to look at John – he was sporting a large smile and nodding his head vigorously.

"In that case, I will see you *tomorrow*, then…" said Lee, depressing the elevator button.

John began to tell his sister about all the *wonderful machines* he had seen today – and he informed her that *every one of them he saw was from his own time!* Freddie smiled contentedly – as this week was going to be just as exciting for John as it was going to be for Alice and himself.

CHAPTER 10

A cold breeze made Alicia's facial muscles tighten as she scowled over the empty hold of Albert's boat. With one hand on the tiller and the other on her hip, she looked every bit the helmswoman. The smile she had started the journey with was still in place as Doris brought her a mug of hot tea. Doris was very pleased with Alicia's change of outlook...it was as if...she was *becoming Alice*...although in Doris' mind, she knew that *her Alice* would be returned to her bosom, and this new Alicia would return to her turbulent times with a new *way of thinking*. Albert had drawn back all the tarpaulins covering the hold as the journey was going to be a short one. Doris had joined him on the opposite side of the boat to help. Alicia had watched this routine that had been perfected over many years...they were like *synchronized dancers* as their arms moved in unison, folding back the heavy covering. Again, this brought the thoughts of her *own parents to mind*...and AGAIN the realization that her father was so *on his own with everything.* In this cold light of day, she could NOT BELIEVE how she had treated her long-suffering father, and just how *evil* her mother really was. It was her *mother* who had sought to *alienate her from her father...in FACT...it was her MOTHER who had ENCOURAGED her to be the way she was!* These thoughts were overtaking her brain as she remembered the bad things she and her mother had plotted against that poor, hard-working man. She tried to find a reason why *anyone* would do this – but the realization that only a hard-nosed, self-centered BITCH could only *think of these things* – never mind actually DOING THEM. Alicia's solitude at the helm was broken by the crowing of a raven flying overhead, as Albert and Doris' synchronized dance drew to a close. Tears welled up in Alicia's eyes and her bottom lip began to quiver, and then smile at the lovely couple who had stolen her gaze. Doris noticed Alicia's eyes first and said, "Whatever is the matter, dear?"

"I was just thinking of how *horrid* I've been...and what a *wonderful life* you and your family share. It is as if a part of me *has died...and another part is being born*...I've never met your Alice, and I'm sure you are *truly thankful for that...but it is like I am beginning to see things as she would!* And the only thing I am worried about now is that when I go back, Alice will leave me, and I will become that horrible, nasty and USELESS excuse of a human being that I used to be!" she sobbed.

"NOW LOOK HERE GIRL!" boomed Albert. "You aren't going through all of this FOR NO REASON! Somebody – or *some thing* –thought you should get a *second chance*...and so far, you are doing *everything right!* I reckon when you go back, nobody will even *recognize you!* Your face may be the same for sure...but the *important thing...what is BEHIND your lovely face...will be totally different!* You will find people will begin to love you for WHO YOU ARE...NOT FOR WHAT YOU HAVE. And then, little Alicia...you will find PEACE and HAPPINESS, the likes of which you have NEVER KNOWN." He continued.

"But what of *Alice?* Surely she will not be learning my ways...that would be *awful!*" answered Alicia.

"Sorry to say this, but there would be no gain for Alice if that was the case...and I don't think the powers that be would do such a thing to such a sweet angel. I believe something *wonderful* is happening for Alice and John...so don't you worry your pretty head about such things. You just concentrate on keeping the boat sure and true. Then, then when you go back, you can live your life the same way." Was Albert's reassuring answer.

Alicia threw her arms as best she could around this great man's girth, burying her head into his chest. Doris smiled and left her man, and ward, as she jumped onto the towpath and walked towards young James to retrieve his tea mug and get him on his feet so the horses could once again begin pulling. The crack of the tightening rope once again sent droplets of water up into the air, and the barge began moving forward.

An hour of effortless gliding over the canal, leaving a gentle wake behind them, brought the great water mill at Thwaite Gate into view, and the coal stage was looming in front of them. Albert jumped off the boat onto the towpath and untied Toby. James led him to a patch of short winter grass. While Toby munched, Albert walked over the bridge to the other side and James coiled up the rope, throwing it to Doris on the barge. As soon as Albert was on the other bank, Doris threw the rope to him so he could pull the barge around. With his mighty arms, Albert began to pull. The bow of the barge began to move starboard, and when it pointed across the canal, Albert began to walk up the towpath towards the coal stage. Doris gave Alicia a rope that was tied to the stern and asked if she would throw it to her. As nimble as a young girl, Doris once again jumped onto the towpath, walked a little ways behind the boat and shouted, "Throw it now!" Alicia threw the rope straight into Doris' awaiting arms. Once again, the husband and wife team worked in *perfect unison*, mooring the boat directly under the coal shute. As all this was happening, James led Toby over the bridge and into place a few strides in front of the barge. Toby again found a small patch of grass to munch on. As soon as the boat was moored, the large man at the coal shute swung the apparatus over the bow hold. As soon as the coal began to load, a *huge plume of black dust engulfed the boat.* Alicia saw it heading *straight for her* at the helm, but there was nothing she could do. It was upon her in an *instant*. She managed to close her eyes with a millisecond to spare. For some strange reason,

A Switch in Time

the only coughing that could be heard was coming from the helm, as Alicia jumped off the boat and onto the towpath, running out from the cloud of dust. Even though she had managed to close her eyes, they were still red and sore as she rubbed them. She could *only imagine* what her normally *beautifully pampered face* looked like now. A few days ago, what had just happened would have sent her into a rage. She looked down at her clothes...she had thought they were shabby before, and now they were *black and dusty*...and she burst into laughter. This was the first time Albert and Doris – or *anyone* for that matter – had heard Alicia laugh this way. Scratching his chin, Albert said, "I should've warned you about that!"

"You did that *on purpose*!" coughed Alicia, still unable to quit laughing.

Albert and Doris, the man at the coal shute, and James all burst simultaneously into gales of laughter with her...and even Toby twitched his ears. The coal flowed quickly from the shute, and when the hold was full, the man wrote down in a book the amount of coal he had despatched, and Albert put his mark upon the document. With three of the crew back on the barge, the fourth member made his clicking sound with his mouth, pulled gently on his rope, and the fifth member of the crew began to pull. This time, after the snapping sound the rope made when taut, there was a *creaking* from the rope as it stretched and the barge began to move ever so slowly.

"What do we do now? Our lovely, clean boat is *filthy again!*" said Alicia.

"Don't worry yer pretty head about that – the wind will have us clean in no time!" said Albert.

To her amazement, she saw that Albert was right, as the settled dust was being blown from not only the boat, but from their clothing too! After an hour of sailing, the coal dust was no more, and all that was left was the slight odour of coal on her clothes. Alicia remembered that *awful thing* she had said about poor

Alice's clothes and felt ashamed of herself. In fact, this strange chain of events was making Alicia *ashamed of every single part of her ridiculously spoilt, useless life.* Her outlook on *everything* was *completely changing* – she began to realize that her brother Jamie's train-set thingie, and the work involved in trying to restore it, was something she should be *complementing for – not ridiculing him for it.* She also realized that her father's business was *something to be proud of*…it wasn't just a *personal bank for her.* Most of all, she could see *beyond a doubt* who was the cause, the creator, of the Frankenstein that she was – her own *mother* was to blame. This thought had been growing in her mind ever since arriving on the barge. Her mother should have been *helping and encouraging her father –* not just taking his money and *spending it* on her personal trainers…with whom she had many *affairs with.* Yes…her mother was a *complete bitch who needed bringing down a peg or two.* This, she swore to herself, *would happen the very day she returned to her own time.*

The wind, now at Alicia's back, helped Toby, as the noble horse towed the now-heavy barge. It wasn't long before they were moored once again outside the same mill where they had moored a couple of days ago.

"We are early!" said Albert. "The job will stop now…" he continued.

"Why?" said Alicia.

"I need your brother back so we can start unloading."

"Show *me* what to do!" offered Alicia with a smile.

"Nay, lass – it's *man's work*." He answered with a chuckle.

"Not in *my time it isn't*! Although I'm not a good example of twenty-first century women, I *do have the right* to do any work that a *man does*!" she announced quite militantly.

"This is a strange time of yours…you can do *anything a man can*…yet all you do back there is *paint your nails*? Seems a *bit daft to me!"* he said.

"Yes...well...as I said, I'm not a typical woman, but that *will change*. Now, *tell me what to do*." She said quite firmly.

"Alright then, young lass, follow me." Replied Albert, placing a heavy shovel in her hand.

The weight of the empty shovel took her by surprise and she lost her balance and fell fully on her bottom on the hard coal. Normally, she would have burst into tears, but there was a *point at stake – and she was going to make the first strike for Women's Liberation whilst Emmeline Pankhurst was still a baby!*

Albert helped her to her feet, looking away, because underwear as Alicia knew it hadn't been invented yet, and her legs were akimbo. This was a thing the old Alicia would have *died from embarrassment from*! Instead, she just said, "I'm sure you've seen *one of those before,* Albert!"

"Not with legs apart like that, and on my *daughter!*" he replied.

Alicia stood up and whispered in his ear, "*I'm not your daughter, remember?*"

"That's true...I was forgetting...you two are *so alike now*...Alice is *always going on about doing John's work*!" said the embarrassed boat-owner.

Smiling, Alicia gave him a wink and said, "Why don't you let her? She might be good at it!"

"Let's see *how you get on first*..." said Albert, as the coal-grabber made its way slowly down to the hold.

"When the grabber gathers the coal and takes it up, we have to make sure there is enough coal in the space where it grabs to get another load...that means we shovel it in." instructed Albert.

The apparatus made a deep hole in the coal, and both Albert and Alicia began shovelling. This was *gruelling work* for Alicia, but she kept her shovel moving. After a while, Jamie returned, and saw his sister *covered in coal dust...with lines of sweat fingering down her face.* He asked what was going on.

"We are emptying the barge…" said an out-of-breath Alicia."

"This I can see…but it's *hard to believe!*" said Jamie. "Do you want me to help?" he continued.

"NO!" screamed Alicia. "WE ARE NEARLY DONE, AND I WANT TO FINISH IT WITH ALBERT!" she continued.

"Alright…I'll go make a pot of tea for us then!" said an amazed Jamie.

Albert took off his flat cap and scratched his head, saying, "Lasses shovelling coal…lads making tea…*the world's turning upside down!*"

Jamie and Alicia burst into laughter. Poor Albert looked bemused, as Jamie climbed down into the barge. Jamie picked up the water jug and filled the kettle. Doris was asleep on her chair, but she woke with a start as Jamie placed the lid back onto the kettle.

"What on *Earth* is going on here?" she asked.

"I'm just making a pot of tea, Doris…would you like one?"

"Stand aside, before you *burn yourself* you *silly man…men making tea…I've never heard the likes of it!*" she grumbled. "Go up top – I'll give you a shout when it's ready…" she continued.

He returned to Albert and Alicia, who were busy shovelling the last of the coal into the large bucket. Jamie was *amazed at his sister…and so PROUD of her*! Albert put his shovel down as the job finished. He looked at Alicia, who was black with coal dust and wet through with sweat, stooped over with her hands on her knees, totally out of breath…but she wore the *broadest grin of satisfaction*. Jamie held out his hand to help his sister exit the boat's hold. When he had helped her on deck, he gave his sister a loving hug and kissed her on her cheek. He told her how proud he was of what she was doing. She smiled at him, enjoying this *sibling intimacy for the first time in her life.*

"Now then, you two...that's enough of all that! Let's go get cleaned up!" interrupted Albert.

"I think that's a good idea!" answered Alicia.

All three of them went downstairs to join Doris and young James.

"C'mon in, you lot, and have this hot tea! Alice...you come over here...let's have that dress, you are filthy!" said Doris.

Alicia walked across to Doris and held her arms up, as would a child. Doris got a hold of the coal-stained garment and lifted it over her head. Alicia, now wearing only a long vest, whispered into Doris' ear, "I'm *Alicia*..."

"It's getting so I can't hardly tell you two apart! It's as if you and her *are the same person!* " said Doris.

"I am *enjoying being like Alice*...and when she returns, she will *live on in me in the twenty-first century*..."

"It's hard for me to understand what is happening, but like Albert, something inside me tells me that this situation is not for long, and everything will work out in the end..." said Doris.

With that, Doris began to wash Alicia's face very gently with a cloth. As the grime was removed from Alicia's face, she smiled at Doris. She had had many facial and beauty treatments...all *kinds of expensive pampering*...but never had she experienced *anything like this*...this was like when she was a little girl, only much better. This was *loving care...the likes of which she had NEVER KNOWN*. When she was a girl, this was performed by a nanny, not her mother...her mother was *far too busy* to do such *mundane tasks*. But here was this woman...who she didn't even really know...*making her feel warm...clean...and LOVED*. She now knew what was missing in her life – the one thing money could not buy. And Doris was lavishing it upon her. Like a bolt from the blue, Alicia suddenly knew what she needed in her life...and it *certainly wasn't money – it was LOVE*. She believed she was already beginning to share it with Jamie, and that felt great! But now, there was a yearning for *deep, caring love…and it engulfed her whole being.*

A Switch in Time

CHAPTER 11

In 2013, Alice was discovering a new kind of love, too. She knew already the love Alicia had just discovered, as she had enjoyed it all her life. She had now found *the love of a gentleman*. This all-encompassing passion for another, that made her laugh, and sing, and *cry* – all at the same time. She had butterflies in her stomach, and she wanted to *scream out loud to the world* of her newfound happiness. For the first time too, she had discovered *physical love*...and all the wonderment, and pain...that it brings. She laid in the bed waiting for her husband to wake. She was just staring at him...and ever-so-gently stroking his hair with her tiny fingers. Freddie awoke, and a beautiful smile awaited him, followed by a loving kiss.

"Good morning, darling!" were Freddie's first words...and Alice had waited over an hour to hear them.

"Good morning, my beautiful Freddie!" was Alice's answer.

The couple arose and exited the bed. Freddie strode over to the wall and slid open a door, which led into the shower. Looking back, he saw Alice was still in the bedroom...he motioned her over, saying, "Come in here, with me..."

"What is it?" she asked.

"It's called a *shower*." Instructed Freddie.

"What? Like a *shower of rain?*" asked Alice.

"Yes, exactly!" he replied. "Come on in!"

This, of course, was the very latest development of electric showers...the type that has jets all the way down the sides, and from above. When Freddie switched it on, Alice screamed out with excitement and surprise.

"This is magic!" she yelped.

"No Alice – it's just a shower." Said Freddie.

Alice's excitement could not be contained as she went running out of the cubicle, and although dripping wet through, ran into the living room where John was still asleep.

"John! John! Wake up! Come with me!" she yelled, dragging him off of the couch.

She told him to take his trousers off, but he wasn't doing it *quick enough*, so she grabbed one of his trouser legs and pulled it down, making him lose his balance. He fell to the floor, and Alice removed his trousers fully. Taking hold of her brother's hand, the naked siblings ran back into the bedroom and into the en-suite shower, where a bemused Freddie was wondering what was going on.

"Get in, John! Before it stops!" shouted Alice.

Now all three of them were standing inside the cubicle. John and Alice were jumping up and down, splashing on the floor and giggling at each other, while Freddie, feeling a little bit strange, stood in the corner of the vast wet-room shower. It didn't take long for him to adjust though, and before long all three of them were clean and refreshed for the day ahead.

Freddie was beginning to lose his inhibitions about his body, as both of his Victorian wards taught him there was *nothing to be ashamed of being naked*.

"What are you going to wear today, Alice?" asked Freddie.

"What a *silly question*!" laughed Alice. "The same as I had on yesterday!

"No, my love…you have LOTS to choose from…we don't wear the same clothes twice…"

"Why not?" she asked.

"We have *much more clothing* these days, and we can wear what we like…it's called *having a wardrobe*…"

"Isn't it a bit silly to have *so many clothes?* However will you wear them all?"

"It's complicated Alice…why women need so many clothes in my time. Now, dry yourself off, and go into that room you went in yesterday, and pick yourself something to wear." Said Freddie.

As Freddie dried himself, he noticed Alice helping her brother get dry before she saw to herself. It was as if her *brother was the child she'd never had.* John, now dry, went back into the living room whilst Alice ran into the walk-in wardrobe. Again, there were *all kinds of clothes*…most brand-new and never worn. Freddie heard shrieks of laughter emanating from Alicia's wardrobe and wondered what was happening. He looked inside to find Alice holding one of Alicia's *ten-thousand pound dresses* that had very little material to it…completely backless, with a tiny strap across the bust, and the skirt was the width of her *father's belt*.

"What is *this* used for?" asked Alice, grinning widely.

"It's one of Alicia's dresses." Answered Freddie.

"This doesn't look like a dress to me…what does she wear it with?"

"Uhhh…nothing at all, probably…knowing her as I do…" he replied.

"You don't like her very much, do you?" asked Alice.

"I *loathe the very ground she struts across.*" Was his honest answer.

"I think she is a *sad girl* if she needs to surround herself with *all this stuff*…I don't need lots of things to make *me* happy…all I need is my family!" Alice observed.

"Well, now, my love – you have *family here*…and more waiting for you when you get back home…" he said a bit sadly.

"I know…and I will *take you back with me in my heart, Freddie…and I will remain faithful to you.*" She replied with a little tear in her eye.

"Now that we have been *bound together eternally…you might find me in YOUR TIME…*" he said hopefully.

"*I think I may have already…when I was a girl…*" she said. She buried her head in his chest and said, "I *love you Freddie Chambers…*"

"*I love you too, Alice.* Right then, Alice Chambers, find yourself something to wear and we shall have breakfast!" said Freddie.

"I like the sound of that name!" she said, as she chose a pair of brand-new white knickers from the drawer. Removing them from their wrapping, she pulled them up her legs until they fit snugly in place. She then pulled on a pair of blue jeans, finishing the look with a yellow crop top.

"The bottom half of this shirt is missing!" announced Alice.

Freddie laughed, saying, "It's *supposed* to look like that!"

"But won't my *belly get cold*?" she asked with trepidation.

"*No, silly*…you will have your coat on!" he giggled.

Alice and Freddie made their way into the living room, where John was already at the table looking at the books Freddie had procured for him.

"*If only I could read…*" John said.

"I can show you a few basic things about reading tonight when you get home…" offered Freddie.

"That would be smashing!" answered John.

"Do you know someone that can read?" Freddie asked.

"I do!" said Alice. "Alf Wheelright can read!"

"Good! Then you will be able to carry on when you get back! Right, then – who wants bacon and eggs?" asked Freddie.

"Me! Me!" was the resounding answer in unison from the Victorians.

Again the siblings tucked into the *wondrous* breakfast of bacon and eggs…but they weren't too bothered about the toast. As breakfast came to a close, the door buzzer sounded – it was Lee Coates calling for John.

Freddie went to the intercom as John flew out of the stairwell door with a piece of bacon in his mouth, muffling the words, "See you later…"

The door slammed shut and an air of calm filled the room.

As Freddie returned to the breakfast table he sat opposite Alice and enquired as to what she would like to do today.

"It is up to you, Freddie! I am in your hands!"

"In that case…would you like to do something from *your century…or something from mine…*" he asked.

"This is a *modern world…there is nothing here from my time…*" she replied.

"Would you like to see some shops from your time?" he asked.

"I've *always wanted to see shops!*" she said excitedly.

"Well that's sorted then! I know exactly where to take you!" he said with a knowing smile.

The loving couple finished their breakfast, tidied away the crockery and made for the elevator. Once outside, Alice linked her arm in Freddie's tightly and asked, "Where are we going?"

"Do you know *Kirkstall Abbey?*" he asked.

A Switch in Time

"*Of course I do, silly!* We have often passed by the Abbey on the barge!" she replied.

"Well, my love – that's where we are going!"

"*Are we going in that taxi thing again? I don't like it – it's scary...*" she muttered.

"I'm afraid so...unless you want to go by bus..." he offered.

"Yes! Yes! The bus...we will go by the bus! Erm...*what's a...bus?*"

"You will see...now, off we go to the bus stop!" he said, grinning at her.

There weren't too many people standing at the bus stop when they arrived, but not long after the bus came along and pulled up at the stop. At first, Alice was afraid when the saw the size of the vehicle...but with gentle coaxing from her beloved Freddie, not only did she board the bus, she climbed the steps to the top deck and sat on the front seat! Freddie purchased their tickets from the driver and went looking for his wife. As he climbed the stairs, he found her at the very front. Much to his amusement, she was standing between the first two seats, with her hands firmly holding the safety bar across the window...as if she was about to begin a journey on a *roller coaster*.

"Come, Alice...sit here by the window, and you can watch our journey as we go..." he offered.

The buses' engine roared into life, as the magic horseless carriage pulled away from the bus stop. Alice tightly squeezed Freddie's hand as forward momentum began. Freddie's firm grip on her eased her fear and she began to get excited, watching everything whiz by so *quickly*. As the bus drove out of Leeds City Centre and along Kirkstall Road, it wasn't too long before the imposing silhouette of *Kirkstall Abbey* could be seen on the horizon. Arriving at their stop outside the abbey the couple left the bus. Abbey House museum was just in front of them. Freddie led Alice by the hand across the busy road, and up the old steps to the quaint little building. Once inside, Alice's eyes *widened* as she saw the street of Victorian shops all in a line. She ran towards the first one and stared in the tiny oblong panes which lined the shop window. She was *amazed* by all the Victorian splendour within the shop. Her heart was beating fast with excitement as she ran from one window to another. There were other people looking around the re-enacted street scene, but they all looked *dull and unimpressed*...but she could not contain her *excitement* as she gazed upon the wonders within. With the broadest smile upon her face, she turned to Freddie. He just stood and watched his sweetheart, his heart swelling with love with *every passing moment.*

"Ohh, Freddie...I have *never seen anything like this...*" she said.

"But...all the shops in *your time* look like this, Alice..."

"I have *never seen a shop in my time...the only time we needed shops, my FATHER saw to it! But I will be going with him next time! I had NO IDEA that shops were this exciting!*" she continued.

"I see...what about John? Has *he* seen shops like this before?" asked Freddie.

"No...this was to be our first trip into Leeds proper!" answered Alice.

"That explains why John was *so excited when he got home* – what he saw in Armley Mills museum must have been a *revelation* to him! I think I might blow your minds tomorrow! I will take you both to *York!*" he said with a grin.

"What's York?" asked Alice.

"It's another city like Leeds...with lots of shops like these you are seeing now...only, you can actually *buy* things there...also, the National Railway Museum is there, and again, I have a very good friend who can show John around, leaving us with a nice romantic day in York!" said Freddie.

A Switch in Time

"How wonderful!" she cried, clapping her hands. "It will be so exciting! Not just for me, but for John! He loves those steam thingies *so much* he won't even know *we aren't there*!" said a very giddy Alice.

At Armley Mills Museum, John and Lee were enjoying a cup of tea.

"Without doubt, I have never met anyone as *keen to learn about the older engines we have here*! What is it that you find so *fascinating about them?"* asked Lee Coates.

"*I just love the sheer power of these engines…I already know some of them have reached speeds of thirty to FORTY miles per hour…which is AMAZING when you think that our boat travels at two to four miles per hour! It must be hard to BREATHE at that speed…"* mused John.

"What do you mean, hard to breathe at forty miles an hour…how fast do you think you were travelling in the *car* on the way here this morning?" Lee asked.

"Umm…I don't know…I had my eyes *closed all the way…*" answered John.

"Why did you have your eyes closed?"

"Everything was going too fast…and there were too many other people going as fast, some even faster than *you! Far too scary for me!*" answered John.

"I see…" said Lee, not quite understanding what was going on.

The two men finished their tea and went back into the museum. Once inside, the curator asked John if he would like to polish some of the brass work on the engines, as Lee had a school class of children to show around. John started polishing straight away, and did so with *gusto*.

Lee went to the door to greet the teachers and children waiting to come inside. As the tour was making its way around the museum, John was still polishing the outer rim of a pressure gauge, when three of the children left the main group and came over to where he was working.

"This *shithole* is *fucking boring*...and you must be a *retard for working here!*" said an eleven year-old boy.

"I don't understand what you are saying." Answered John.

"See...I *told you...he's a fucking retard!* SHUT UP YOU TWAT!" said the boy again...only this time he spit on the engine John was working on.

John could not understand what was going on. He asked the boy why he did that. The boy just answered, "*Shut the FUCK UP, RETARD...AND GET ON WITH YOUR JOB.*"

John called over to Lee, and he came over to where John was working.

"Can you help me here? I am not understanding what these boys are saying to me."

"*Why? What are they saying?*" asked Audrey Lawler, the class form teacher.

"I don't understand the words *fucking, retard, twat and shut the fuck up*...also, I don't understand why he had to *spit* on this lovely machine..." said John to the shocked form teacher.

"HOW DARE YOU USE SUCH FOUL LANGUAGE IN FRONT OF THESE LOVELY CHILDREN? YOU OUGHT TO BE ASHAMED OF YOURSELF!" screeched Audrey Lawler.

"Now now...let's all *keep calm and work this out."* Said Lee. "I'm *sure* it's a misunderstanding, so let's carry on with the tour. And *teacher*...kindly *keep your children UNDER CONTROL*...because I did overhear the boy *abusing my employee*...and if this goes any further, I shall CEASE ALLOWING ALL THE SCHOOLS OF LEEDS INTO THIS MUSEUM!" he continued in a very stern voice, his face a stony wall of seriousness.

A Switch in Time

The teacher looked *stunned* that one of her 'little angel' knew such language and said, "If the boy *did say such things*, it is because he has had a *hard life*. I was talking to him only the other day, and found out he is the only boy in his class that doesn't have a *Playstation 3*. He has to make due with a Playstation 2 knowing that everybody else has the better one! In this day and age, that is a *hard thing for children to deal with...and this man here probably knows nothing of SUFFERING, and should have known BETTER than to REPEAT THOSE AWFUL WORDS!*"

"What is a 'play station'?" asked John.

"Are you *trying to provoke me??*" asked the teacher.

"I don't know what that means either." Said John in all seriousness.

"C'mon children...we are leaving. Let us all get back on the bus and forget we *ever came here!*" announced Audrey.

As the bus pulled away, all the children on the back seat were pointing their middle fingers upwards at the two man standing in the door.

"Why did you have to repeat what the children said, John?" asked Lee.

"Because I *didn't understand what those words meant – I've never heard them before...*" John replied.

"You must live on a *desert island* in that case. Nowadays these words are common, everyday words that we have to put up with!" said Lee, not believing what he was hearing.

"I live on a *canal boat...*" said a puzzled John.

Lee Coats just looked at John and realized, this conversation was *getting nowhere*. He thought to himself that maybe John had a learning disability or special needs – so he took the conversation no further.

106

Lee placed his arm around John's shoulder and took him back inside. He declared that it must by now be dinnertime, so the two took their dinner break.

It was also dinnertime at Kirkstall Abbey, and outside stood a *burger van.*

"Perfect! This is *just the thing to keep us warm! A nice hot burger and chips!*" exclaimed Freddie.

"It smells *lovely...*" observed Alice.

Freddie ordered two lots of burgers and chips and the couple sat at a picnic table beside the van.

Alice had overheard the lady serving the food say, "That will be *seven pounds, please...*" and asked what she had been talking about.

"That's how much the burgers cost." Replied Freddie.

"How can that be? Seven pounds...*such a lot of money!*" marvelled Alice.

"Back in *your time*, seven pounds *is a lot of money*...but in 2013 it isn't." he replied.

"In my time, or *yours*...I could *never even THINK of spending SEVEN POUNDS on TWO MEALS!*"

"It's just the difference in time, that's all...I couldn't imagine trying to live like you and your family do, just in the same way you couldn't live like we do here." He said.

After eating just a quarter of her meal, she was full and began to wrap the burger up to take home for John.

"What are you doing, Alice?" enquired Freddie.

Alice informed him of her plan.

"There is no need to do that, sweetheart! If John wants a burger when he gets home, I will have him one delivered!"

"We can't let this *go to waste, Freddie! There is an awful lot of food here...we must take it home with us and eat it later!*" she said, surprised.

"There is *no need for that Alice – we have plenty of food at time.*"

"That's NOT THE POINT! You cannot leave food when there are so many *starving children on the canal!*" she stared agog.

"The thing is...there *aren't* any starving kids on the canal anymore...most of the people that live by canals are quite *well off*..it is totally different now, my love..." he reassured her.

"Are things *so changed in the future that you can throw away PERFECTLY GOOD FOOD...and not FEEL ASHAMED? I was taught from an early age it is a SIN to waste food! In my time...people sometimes go for DAYS without food...I can't suddenly FORGET ALL THAT, Freddie!*" she said anxiously.

"Of course you can't, Alice, and I wouldn't expect you to. You, of course, are absolutely *right* – it is wrong to waste food. Too much of what we do in this century is wrong. There may be better housing, and hospitals, but there is corruption *everywhere*. In many ways, your simpler way of living is *far better* than what we have today." Comforted Freddie.

A little smile came back to Alice's face and she threw her arms around him and gave him a big kiss.

"Let's not argue anymore, my handsome gentleman. What shall we do now?" she asked excitedly.

"We could go for a walk along the canal..."

"I've done that *loads of times!*" she interrupted.

"In that case, we could head back to the penthouse and pass the time away until John arrives home..." said Freddie with a knowing wink.

"What's wrong with your eye, Freddie?" she asked.

John Paul Bernett

"There's nothing wrong with my eye…I mean…would you like to do what we did yesterday?" he said with a little smile.

"Oh, I see….YES PLEASE!" was her quick reply.

"In that case, let's catch the bus!" he said.

The happy couple left the Abbey House Museum and made their way to the bus stop. The journey back to the penthouse for Freddie was uneventful. He didn't see all the trees…the church spires…the birds…or even the people going about their daily tasks, because he was used to it, so he paid it no mind. Alice, on the other hand, was to coin a phrase, 'in Wonderland'…all the bright colours that made up Freddie's world were *sparkling* to Alice, and the grin on her face through the whole journey paid testament to that.

After a short walk from the bus, it had gotten to three o'clock already, but they were home. Freddie put the kettle on whilst Alice collapsed on the luxurious sofa.

"I've had the *best time ever*." Said Alice.

"Me too!" he said as he brought the tea in from the kitchen.

"What now?" she said, with a cheeky grin.

"The *removal of your clothing*, methinks…" said Freddie as he put his cup down. "John won't be back for a couple of hours, so we will have the place to ourselves."

"What does that matter?" she asked.

"We don't want him to catch us *making love*, do we?" asked Freddie.

"You *are* silly! What does it matter? Our mom and dad used to do it all the time…and NOW I know what they were doing! It's not like it is something *wrong*…is it?" answered Alice.

Once again, Alice had pointed out a truth that Freddie's world didn't live by – and he knew she was right. If John *were* to come in and catch them both naked and making love, he would probably walk up to them and *tell him about his day.* With that thought, Freddie chuckled and said, "*I love you, Alice...*" and began removing her clothes, which he did very slowly and quite deliberately.

Alice lay back and let her man undress her. Once again she was *tingling all over.* This was the part she had begun to *cherish*...made more special to her because she had decided this was *her time*, and she was *going to enjoy it.* The undressing and the naked kissing and cuddling were the *best part* for her. The physical love was harder, for it caused her discomfort. She tried to hide this, but Freddie had noticed her pained expression and had asked her, "*Is this hurting you?*"

Alice looked up at him and said, "I think it's because I've been a virgin for too long...but you keep going, because I want to please you."

As soon as those words had left her lips, Freddie, being the gentleman that he was, withdrew immediately. "My darling...you should have said...*what a beast I've been...*" he said, upset with himself.

"NO YOU HAVEN'T! Normally, people have plenty of time for these sorts of things...but we *don't. You just carry on, Freddie...*" said Alice.

"There are *many ways of pleasuring a woman, Alice...I don't need to hurt you inside. Instead of using my...uh...I could use my...tongue? Remember that feeling you got when I kissed you there?*"

She eagerly nodded her head in anticipation as Freddie's mouth kissed its way down to her quite small honey-pot of pleasure. With the very tip of his tongue, he thrilled her. Alice shuddered as her excitement mounted, and as she learned *even more* about physical love – and about what it meant to be with a *true gentleman.* Their afternoon of love, although different to the previous day's, was just as rewarding. Alice was laying on the bed with flushed cheeks and a rosy flush along her chest too. Her breasts were heaving, and neither of them could talk. The late afternoon melted away like the mid-winter sun as Alice and Freddie lay in satiated slumber, both entwined on the sofa, at total peace with the world. Then the buzzer rudely awoke them again.

"I will get it..." Freddie sighed as he stumbled to the intercom.

It was John and Lee.

"C'mon up!" he said.

Both Alice and Freddie put on dressing gowns as the elevator arrived.

"Hi guys!" said Freddie. Lee answered, but John didn't seem his usual self.

"What's the matter, John?" asked Alice, as she led him by the arm into the other room.

"Can I have a quick word, Freddie?" asked Lee.

"Of course! There's nothing wrong...is there?"

When Alice and John had disappeared into the bedroom, Lee asked, "Is there something you're not telling me about this boy?"

"What do you mean?"

"I can't put my finger on it! He looks upon my machines as if they are some sort of new technology – he knows *nothing* of current affairs...and this morning, he had *no idea* that a *child was taking the piss out of him!*" said a concerned Lee.

"Oh – I see...do you know what *Amish* is?" Freddie asked.

"Those people in America that shun the modern world?" replied Lee.

"That's right...well, that is what *these two are* – so, I suppose it *is* new technology to them. So, if a kid was swearing at him, he

A Switch in Time

simply would not have understood him..." said Freddie, lying through his teeth.

"*Thank GOD for that!* Well, that certainly would explain it! Oh....shit! I think I said the word *fuck* in front of him today!" said Lee.

"It's okay...he wouldn't have known that word *at all.* Oh, by the way, I need him tomorrow – I'm taking them both to York tomorrow."

"No problem! I shall pick him up the day after, then!"

When the elevator doors closed, Freddie went into the bedroom and joined Alice and John.

"Heyyy, John! I've just asked Lee not to come tomorrow, because Alice and I have a *surprise for you*!" he announced with a broad grin.

John looked quite dejected as he stared back at Freddie.

"*He thinks he's let everybody down...*" explained Alice.

"What makes you think that, John?" asked Freddie.

"I behaved *badly* today, I think..." answered John.

"NONSENSE!" exclaimed Freddie. "Lee told me what happened, and he puts *all the blame on those school children, so cheer yourself up, because you are going to the NATIONAL RAILWAY MUSEUM IN YORK TOMORROW!*"

John's face lit up with excitement, but then he realized how long it would take to get there. "It will take FOREVER!"

"About three-quarters of an hour." Said Freddie.

"WHAT?" said the siblings in unison, their looks of disbelief almost matching.

"You will see tomorrow, when we go to the train station..." Freddie answered.

He gave John a reassuring smile and walked back into the living room. He opened the door to the balcony and stepped outside. Astronomy was a keen interest of his, and he noticed it was a cloudless sky. Although the lights of Leeds diminished his view somewhat – it was still a beautiful starry night. Looking up at the stars – differently this time, because this was the first time he was a *lover* admiring their magnificence – a warm glow filled his heart…tinged with the sadness of knowing *it would all soon be over…and he would never see Alice again.*

A Switch in Time

CHAPTER 12

Doris had tied Alicia's hair back, and the twenty-first century girl stood there in a long vest, and in that simplicity, she looked as pretty as a picture.

"Now, then!" said Albert. "Look at you, stood there like a princess! Come and give your old dad a kiss..."

"Thank you, kind sir..." she said, giving him a curtsey and planting a kiss on his cheek.

Jamie put his arms around her and asked, "Is it *really you*?"

"Ohhhh...I do hope so, Jamie – there is *so much to put right when I get back home*...that being said, this feels more like home than our mansion *ever did* – and I now know why you shunned it. I'm also thinking of *all the nasty things I've called Freddie Chambers*..." she said.

"Don't worry too much over Freddie – he's had one or two names for you, too!" laughed Jamie.

"Yes...but he had *good cause to call me names*...I did not. I scorned him because he wasn't rich." Said Alicia.

"Freddie Chambers, did you say, Alice?" enquired Albert. "He has been in my mind a lot since you two arrived..."

"How so, Albert? Freddie Chambers is my *closest friend in the 21st century*!" exclaimed Jamie.

"He may be lad – but Alice had a friend called Freddie Chambers when she was a young'un...inseparable, they were – they did everything together. She was only four or five, and won't remember him now – but there was *something about that lad*...he was like a beanpole, tall and thin, as I recall – but why I should remember him now, I have no idea…he's been dead *years*…" said Albert.

"Oh, that's sad, Albert! How did he die?" Alicia asked.

"Diphtheria got him when he was six…him and a lot of others, as I recall. We lost two of ours to the same thing." Albert answered.

"You have lost *two of your children, Albert?*" asked Alicia, her eyes beginning to well up again.

"Two during that time, but all told we've lost *five*…three at childbirth and the other two I just told you about." Albert sighed.

Alicia struggled to think how these people *dealt with the life they had*…and how *steadfast in their happiness they were!* The realization was to Alicia that money *really was the root of all evil*. Again, thoughts of her father without the love or respect of a daughter intruded. He wasn't a *rich man at all* – although he was the wealthiest person Alicia had ever met, when it came to *receiving love…her father was a PAUPER.* He worked just as hard as Albert…his working hours just as long…yet he never indulged himself with any luxuries. Luxuries were *lavished upon his wife and daughter*…mostly without his knowledge. Alicia's father was a *very poor man indeed*…and Albert, he was a RICH MAN – with the love of an *entire family*. Now that she had sorted that out, her head became clearer, her future path becoming set in her mind. Jamie, however, was in a thoughtful mood. The coincidence of Alice's friend's name turning over and over in his mind…was there a *link?* He couldn't rule it out, because he was *already in the middle of an impossible scenario – so, surely, ANYTHING WAS POSSIBLE.* So 'why' was the question. The thought that entered Jamie's mind was, had his long-term friendship been made solely to get him to this point in his life, at this *specific time?* If so, to what reason? *Was it a reason to be dealt with in THIS CENTURY – OR IN THE 21ST? Could it be BOTH CENTURIES?* His concentration was broken by the voice of his sister.

"A penny for them?" she asked.

"As if you would bother with a penny!" answered Jamie.

The two siblings laughed simultaneously as the mood in the room grew lighter.

"Right, then! That's enough for sad talk! There's *no wage for turning over old stones!*" said Albert, as he removed from a little cupboard an old squeezebox, and began to play a tune.

Doris began to sing along, and young James began to clap his hands. The whole mood lifted to the tapping of Albert's foot. After a while, Alicia said she was going topside for a little fresh air. Once there, she noticed the sky was clear...they were moored just outside the smog of Leeds. The stars were *beautiful on that crisp winter's evening*...and as she looked at them, her mind wondered, *was anyone she knew looking at these same stars in her time? Did anyone miss her?* Unfortunately, she knew the answer – and it made her very sad.

The next day started in the usual way, with Doris and Alicia rising first. Alicia went straight outside to collect some kindling, and was pleased to see that it hadn't been as cold, so, hopefully there would be no bad surprises for her this morning. There were no such horrors – but there *was* a middle-aged woman walking up the towpath towards her.

"Good mornin', me dearie..." said the woman in rags. Alicia noticed she was carrying a small child.

"Good morning." She answered.

"You have a *kind face*..." said the woman. "I haven't eaten in days...could you spare some food for the baby and me?" she uttered.

Alicia was shocked at how thin they both were. "I don't have anything...I'm sorry...but I do have *this*..." she said, tugging off her finger the gold ring her mother had given her for her 18th birthday. It was a family heirloom, and had belonged originally to her great-great-grandmother, who had passed it down through a procession of female family members. The woman took it from her and asked, "Do I *know you?* Your face – *it seems familiar to me…*"

"I don't think so, I'm not from around here…I'm just visiting." Alicia replied.

"Maybe this ring might change my luck! I will keep it forever…there is something *strangely familiar about you…I think you might be my Guardian Angel…Yes! That's what you are, with your kind face and helpful ways…thank you ever so much!*" said the thin little lady as she scurried off.

Alicia was moved by what had just transpired, and on the way back to the barge, she thought back to her 18th birthday, and the conversation she had had with her mother. Then Doris shouted her name.

"Yes, Doris, I'm here!" she shouted back.

"What did *she want…*the *common prostitute…*" asked Doris.

"She wanted to know if I had any food – I told her I had none."

"Good! She's a good-for-nothing strumpet! Did she ask you to take the child?"

"No! Why would you ask me that?" Alicia asked, surprised.

"Well…me and that woman go back a long way. I can tell *you* because you will never meet Alice. Albert and me had been wed for *three years and still no young'un…*we were *beginning to think one would never come, when I met the woman you just met* – *28 years ago this VERY WEEK. Let's just say…she had a 'business opportunity' for me.*"

"She sold you *her baby?*" marvelled Alicia.

"Yes, she did. She sold me that little baby for a *sixpence*…but no mention of this to ANYONE, mind! Alice is as much *our child* as if I had bore her myself…and NOTHING will ever change that!"

Alicia put her arms around her surrogate mother and squeezed her ever-so-gently, as she whispered in Doris' ear, "*Your secret is safe with me."*

It was only when the two ladies got back to the barge and the men were fed that Alicia began thinking again of her 18th birthday, and that conversation with her mother. The conversation was about how the ring had come into the family in the first place. Her great-great-grandmother had had the ring *given to her by an ANGEL* – and the ring had *brought her luck*. Of course, the family thought the old girl was insane…but the story had been passed down through the generations. Alicia just sat back in her chair and thought…*I was that angel*…she felt a shudder go through her body…but then a ripple of laughter as she realized the better-than-everybody *Alicia* and even funnier, her *mother*, had *descended from a common prostitute.*

In the 21st century, the winter sun was shining again, and three ordinary-looking people blended in with every else at Leeds City Station. Two of them, however, grabbed hold of their rather taller companion's hands every time a train arrived. It wasn't long before the train to York pulled alongside their platform. Droves of people flooded out from the train. This was the *largest crowd* the Victorian siblings had ever seen, and they held onto Freddie's hands for dear life. Freddie just laughed and said, "Come on inside." Very reluctantly, they climbed into the carriage, and John steered them towards a table seat. Alice and John each grabbed a window seat.

"I thought you two were scared!" said Freddie.

"It's not as noisy in here." Replied Alice.

John, like Alice, for the first time in his life was sitting on a *train*…and his excitement gained momentum along with the train pulling out of the station. Both John and Alice sat back in their seats in shock when a voice came over the PA system giving information about their route.

"It's okayyy, guys – it's just the guard telling us where the train will be stopping en route."

After they pulled out of Leeds, the train picked up speed. The look on the two Victorian's faces was *priceless*. For thirty minutes, they kept their eyes closed…all the way to York Station, and then with Freddie exited the carriage. Unlike Leeds Station, this was the type of civil engineering that John had witnessed before along the canal with the giant warehouses. Again, the amount of people rushing past was quite frightening, as Alice and John kept themselves very close to Freddie.

On leaving the station, John and Alice again stepped into a new world. Alice said to John, "Look, there! Kirkstall Abbey isn't in *ruins*! The giant can't have sat on that one!"

"*Giant?*" said Freddie with a puzzled expression.

John laughed and said, "It's what my pa used to tell us whenever we passed Kirkstall Abbey – he would say, 'look, John boy, the Abbey looks like that because a *giant once stopped there and sat on the roof!*'"

"It's true!" exclaimed Alice, sporting a pout as she crossed her arms.

"I'm not too sure about that part of history to know." Said a diplomatic Freddie.

"It *was a giant…*" muttered Alice as she stuck her tongue out at her brother.

Soon they had followed the road around to the left and walked the short distance to the British Railway Museum. Once there, John was eager to start…but they had to wait for Freddie's friend Bob Jones to arrive at reception.

"Hello, Freddie!" said Bob. Freddie smiled and shook his hand.

"Hello, Bob! This is John, who we spoke of…"

"Good morning John! Are you ready for your guided tour?" Bob asked.

Whilst still shaking hands, John's head was nodding at a great pace.

"I will leave him in your capable hands, Bob." Said Freddie, as he took Alice's hand and said, "See ya later, John!"

Both Freddie and Alice waved and left together.

"Well then, John – where would you like to start?" asked Bob.

"Mr. Coates told me you have a *Stephenson's Rocket* – can I see that one, please? I don't know what one is, so I am quite eager to see it!" he replied.

"*You don't know what the Rocket is?*" gaped Bob.

"No sir." John replied.

"In that case, we shall start there – we have two; a working replica, and one showing the inside workings of the engine…" replied Bob, leading the way to the most famous steam locomotive in history.

Outside the museum, Fred and Alice strolled down the road, and through one of the giant doorways that leads you through the great city wall.

"What would you like to do first?" Freddie asked.

"I don't know! I'm too excited!" replied Alice.

With a knowing smile, Freddie led Alice to a row of waiting horse-drawn carriages, and helped her up into the first one in line. Alice clapped her hands with glee when she sat upon the buttoned leather seat. Freddie sat alongside, and to a sound similar to what young James made for Toby, the horse effortlessly pulled away.

Back in the 19th century, Alicia had been thoughtful for quite some time, when Doris said, "You're quiet, little Alice…"

Laughing, Alicia said, "I'm *Alicia*…"

"I don't know – it's getting harder to tell you two apart! When you first came here, you didn't resemble her likeness at all – but then, you started to smile a little…and in a *certain light*, you looked a bit like her. But now – now, *your face seems to have changed* – no…*changed* is the wrong word, your face has become *more relaxed*, and now, you and my sweet Alice are *identical*…" mused Doris.

"I think I know what you mean, Doris – I *feel different* – I'm not as *tense*. When you don't have to be *better* than someone else, it seems like the pressure has been taken off of you. Maybe, this is the *real me*…and the other me was what I had been *turned into*. Not that I am making any excuses for myself! I was a *completely spoiled bitch*! It does not make sense to the *old Alicia*…but I am *so much happier here…now*…than I was in the future."

"So – what *were* you thinking about?" asked Albert, as he had heard most of the conversation from the helm.

"I have a *ring*…for some reason, it is the *only thing that came with me*. It is a *family heirloom*, and I received it for my 18th birthday. My great-great…ohhh I don't know how many greats, but you know what I mean…*grandmother*…was supposed to have been given this ring…*by an angel*…the thing is, the woman I have just given it to looked at me *very strangely*, and said, '*You are an angel, and I will never forget your kindness*' – and a cold shiver went through my body…" said Alicia.

"Well, lass, not that I know ought about this sort of thing, but if it's *my thoughts on the matter you want*, they are this: That fine brother of yours has come here to get my John and Alice on something that's to do with the '*future*', as you call it. *You* have come here to find out what happened in *your past*. Also, you needed to find out what is *important in life*, and that, my girl, is *family* – and a good 'hoss."

"You're right about the family, Albert, but as to the *horse*...I have *three of those that I haven't even SEEN in over a year...*" said Alicia regretfully.

"THREE 'HOSSES!? BLOODY 'ELL GIRL, HOW RICH IS THA FATHER??" Enquired Albert.

"At the last count, his personal wealth was around 99 *million*..." she answered honestly.

"I don't know what that is...but I once saw a rich main holding a sovereign..." replied Albert.

"To give you an idea, Albert, my father probably has more money than there is in the entire country today." Quipped Alicia.

"Did you 'ere that, Doris?? Well, Alicia, your father must be a man to *look up to*!" said Albert.

"You are right, Albert – he must be. I am beginning to think he is your great-great-grandson, or something like that." Alicia said.

"That could be true, lass – *I could be the start of the 'Watson Empire'*" said Albert with a laugh.

"The only thing is...we are called *Winters*..." said Alicia.

"Happen that's how it was! Happen maybe somebody only had *girls* along the line..." mused Doris.

"You can't have a company name that's a *girl's name, Doris!*" corrected Albert.

"Not NOW we can't...but it sounds like we might be able to in this 'future' we've heard about!" said Doris.

"Lasses running businesses? I've never heard the like!" answered Albert.

"In the *future*, Albert, there has been a lass *Prime Minister*..." said Alicia.

A Switch in Time

Poor Albert just shook his head and said, "*Mark my words – these women will be wanting to VOTE soon!*"

"I don't think you need to worry about that for another twenty years or so." Comforted Alicia.

The two ladies laughed at Albert's bemused expression, as she said, "Well I'm going topside! I can't spend the whole day *talking* like you women do!"

Again, the ladies just burst into laughter.

Jamie was sweeping the factory floor when four young lads that worked there pulled him roughly into an adjacent stock room and began pushing him around. The tallest one of them got hold of him by his collar and pulled it tight, saying, "*So you're the new apprentice – there are ONE OR TWO THINGS you need to KNOW – firstly, every morning you GIVE ME YOUR DINNER, and EVERY WEEK YOU GIVE ME A PENNY OUT OF YOUR WAGE.*"

"Do I just give a penny to you, or *all of you?*" enquired Jamie.

"Just ME." Said the loutish boy.

"In that case, we don't *need* the rest of you…" said Jamie, giving the three lads standing together a *roundhouse kick*, connecting each one on the chin, sending them instantly to the floor, profusely bleeding.

"Now. I think we will *re-negotiate our deal.*" Said Jamie. The yob looked *stunned.* "Every morning, when I walk in, *you and only you* will have a pot of tea awaiting *my arrival!*"

The boy reached back as if he was going to strike Jamie – but once again, his old karate training his father had made him take paid off, with a perfectly-landed punch to the jaw. The boy hit the dirt, joining his friends, who were only now coming to. They all managed to stagger to their feet, and Jamie said to the leader, "Do we have an accord?"

"Yes sir – please don't hit me again…" begged the leader.

All four of them exited the room bleeding and dazed. Following behind was an unscathed Jamie, who picked up his broom and carried on sweeping. The Works Foreman walked over to Jamie and said, "What has just taken place?"

"Those young men have just let me know who is in charge, sir." Replied Jamie.

The foreman looked at the dazed and bleeding ruffians and said, "So I see...carry on, young man."

Jamie spent the rest of the day in the drawing office, as he had been told it needed tidying up whilst the engineer was away. This, of course, was a *dream opportunity* for Jamie to do some work for himself. He began surveying the plans for all the different engines they had, and sure enough, the plans for his own engine were there. It was an older engine, and was no longer in production...so he *hatched a plan.* This drawing had *everything on it he needed to know about his old engine*; he folded it up and put it in an empty tin box the size of a biscuit tin, placing it underneath his jacket. Going back downstairs, he told the foreman he had finished, and was it okay to finish the bricklaying he had begun the other day? The foreman happily agreed and Jamie descended the ladder into the cellar. Quickly walking to the wall he had rebuilt, he picked up the hammer and chisel that were still down there. He knocked out the mortar between four of the bricks and removed them. He then with the chisel split the bricks so the box would fit in the space behind them. He then placed the box in the gap, and then put the fascias of the bricks and the mortar back in place, so it would remain there until he got back and showed Freddie his great discovery. Feeling very happy with himself, he climbed back up the ladder and into the workroom.

In York, John was seeing the marvel of his age – *Stephenson's Rocket.* Most people are pleased to see the rocket, but John looked like he was viewing the latest *Ferrari.* He had walked past quite a few locomotives as he strolled along with Bob Jones, but had not recognized them as *steam engines*. He even walked right past the *Mallard* without batting an eyelid…but the sight of the Rocket made him *euphoric.*

"Do you have some paper and a pencil, so I can make a drawing to show my dad?" enthused John.

"I'll tell you what – as you are a friend of Freddie's, you can take a photo of it with your phone…"

John Watson just gaped at him and said, "I don't understand your words, sir…*phone…photo…*what are these things?"

Bob Jones just scratched his head, looking very bemused. "I will get you some drawing paper…" he said.

The horse and carriage ride was just as exciting for Alice as the Railway Museum was for John. "I wish this could last forever!" she said.

So did Freddie. But he knew with each passing day, this wonderful life was *drawing to a close.* He could *not believe how quickly someone could fall in love, as he had. He felt he was the LUCKIEST MAN IN EXISTENCE – but also, the unluckiest. He knew he would have to give her up and return to his old life, of which he used to think was perfect. He now knew it was not. He looked at Alice and how she was taking in everything she saw with the biggest sweet smile on her face. He realized, she was building a LIFETIME OF MEMORIES from which she could draw upon for the REST OF HER LIFE. Freddie for some reason could not think that way…his train of thought was quite different. He had wondered, for a moment, if they might meet again in this life. He knew they had not already met, because not only had Alice taken his virginity, she was his first real girlfriend. So would there come a day when she might walk back into his life? He also knew SHE would be different, as she would have been brought up in this DAY AND AGE – and her beautiful innocence would have been lost.*

John Watson was now very excited – pencil in hand – drawing this wonder of the age. Bob Jones had left him to it, as he went outside to check on the Rocket's facsimile – and just as he had thought, it was in steam. Arriving back at the cut-away version of this wondrous engine of the past, he found John finishing up his drawing.

"Okay John – I have a surprise for you!" said Bob.

John's face beamed with a smile as he was led outside of the museum to the full-sized replica, in full steam, *Stephenson's Rocket.* John ran towards the wonder of his age.

"Well, John? What are you waiting for? Hop on, and let's go for a ride!"

John's face lit up with the biggest smile Bob had ever seen as he leapt onto the foot plate. To be standing where he was was beyond his *wildest dreams.* He had only heard rumours of its greatness – and now he was actually standing on the foot plate of what up until now had been only a dream. The blowing of a coach horn signalled the start of the journey, and John held on with all his might. The experience was *exhilarating, as John was at least where he wanted to be.* He was *riding the future* – IN THE FUTURE…and he new NOTHING would EVER BE THE SAME AGAIN.

A Switch in Time

CHAPTER 13

In the 19th century, Alicia's and Jamie's work day had begun. Alicia's journey was going to be slightly longer today, as they were going on what Albert called the 'Abbey Haul'. This journey would take them from Thwaite Gate to Kirkstall. As Toby began to pull the fully-laden barge, Alicia was the first at the tiller, covered in coal dust, coughing and wiping her eyes. It was yet another cold but clear day...well, clear in as there were no *clouds in the sky*...but the smoke from the chimneys had already begun darkening the day. Alicia had taken to steering the boat like a duck to water. Albert had a bit more time on his overworked hands, so he pulled out his squeezebox and played a little tune. Without realizing what she was doing, Alicia was at first *humming along...and then SINGING the words of the song as he was playing.*

"Now how do you know the words, Alicia? That is a song that I *made up and used to sing to the young'uns at bedtime!*"

"I don't know, Albert – I just *know the song*...Yes! My father used to sing it to me...I had forgotten he used to do that!" Alicia replied.

So, with young James out in the front with Toby and Doris below deck having 40 winks, the happy little canal boat *Lightning* was pulled along the canal towards Kirkstall, with its crew singing.

When Jamie arrived at work that morning, he called in to see the man in charge of the steam engine. This had become a routine, as he had struck up a friendship with him. He was also learning from this man about what he listens for, because apart from the oiling, that was the most important thing about running a steam engine. His friend would tell him about the different *hisses and groans*...but when he heard something that was *different,* he would immediately attend to it. Jamie took in *every single word from this man from the distant past.* The morning went quite smoothly – no kung fu – just a nice steaming pot of tea when he arrived, and a day doing bits and bobs. Jamie asked the foreman what the cellar was actually used for.

"Inquisitive little bugger, aren't ye lad?" said the foreman.

"Yes sir, I want to do well here..." replied Jamie.

"Seems to me 'thas a quick learner...the way you dealt with those young lads yesterday was quite impressive."

"I hope you won't hold that against me, sir."

"Of course not! I can't be doing with loafers, softies or telltales...you handled yourself *correctly* in my opinion, and no more needs to be said on the subject."

"Pardon, sir – but...the cellar??"

"Ah yes – we tried to use it for *casting*...the furnace is still down there – it's bricked up behind the opposite wall to the one you fixed. All the mouldings are still under the stone flags – we couldn't get it to work proper – so the engineer had it all covered up until later. He then found he could have it done elsewhere, and it was cheaper too, so it just all...stayed buried, so to speak..."

"Thank you very much, Sir." Said Jamie, trying to hold back his ecstatic self. This, to Jamie, was like *finding the Holy Grail* – all the mouldings for the parts he needed were still probably lying in pristine condition under the floor in the 21st century! He began to think that this strange trip was not only for his sister, and his contemporary from the 19th century, it held *wonderful repercussions* for himself, too! Knowing this, he wondered what possibly could *Alice* gain from this...after all, she was living the life of his *sister,* poor thing! With the knowledge of his new find tucked away in his memory for another time, he set about his daily task of making a *new life for John Watson.*

Jamie's up-until-now spoilt *waste of space sister* was singing along to Albert's squeeze box as she safely negotiated Albert's pride and joy through the lock and onto the part of the *River Aire* that ran past her 21st century penthouse. Looking up, she pointed it out to Albert.

"Look, Albert – that's where I live!"

"You live in a *mucky old factory?"* was his surprised answer.

"Nooo...that *other Alicia wouldn't know what a 'mucky factory'* was! I own the *entire top floor of that building.* It has been turned into *luxury apartments!"* She then corrected herself and said, *"Places to live..."*

"There must be a lot of you for you all to fill that space!" replied Albert.

"No, Albert – just *me..."* she answered, hanging her head in shame.

"It's good that there is housing for *everyone* in your day lass, if that is an abode for one!"

Feeling even more ashamed she said, "Albert – there are *whole families that don't have ANYWHERE to live – and we have young people LIVING ON THE STREETS IN BOXES...*"

"I can't see the sense in that, Alicia – if there is enough room for one person to live in a space that *twelve families could live in*, why isn't there enough housing for everyone else?"

"Because of *people like me*, wanting more and more – and not giving a *shit* about people's *needs*. My time is all about wanting stuff – and *wanting it NOW.* I'm ashamed to be a part of it – I wish I could stay *here...*"

"Na'then lass – we'll have a bit less *profanity*. What's this about *staying here*? How can you *change anything by staying here? You wouldn't want to condemn Alice to your life – would you?"*

More and more, Alicia was discovering *new things about herself...and realizing what a PARASITE she really was...the words CONDEMN ALICE rang out loud and clear.*

"You are *absolutely right,* Albert...no...I wouldn't want to condemn poor Alice to my life. Things *do need to change when I get back. I am going to be a VERY BUSY girl – and a WHOLE LOT OF PEOPLE AREN'T GOING TO LIKE IT!*"

Albert nodded his head and gave one of his knowing smiles as the barge sailed past the building with Toby pulling them on towards Kirkstall.

On arriving at the coal stage in between Kirkstall and Horsforth, Toby was pulled to a halt by young James, and Alicia leapt off the stern with the rope. She quickly wrapped it around the mooring tie holding onto the end of it. The rope tightened, and three turns around the peg took the strain, with the fully-laden barge coming to a stop. Running up to the bow, she shouted to Albert to throw her the bow rope and she repeated her actions at the mooring of the bow, tying the barge up quickly and skilfully. It wasn't long before Albert and Alicia were hard at work moving the coal from the bow hold. Alicia wiped the coal dust-soaked sweat from her brow and said, "At least I didn't waste my time at the gym, it has certainly prepared me for this!"

"Who's this *Jim*?" asked Albert.

Alicia laughed and said, "The *gymnasium* is a place where you work your muscles to get fit."

"Hard work does that!" replied Albert.

"Yes it does, but in my time it's a *leisure activity*. You walk on a treadmill, and you *lift weights to tone your muscles*."

Albert shook his head, saying, "I can't believe you still subject the orphan children to that!"

"No, Albert, workhouses are long gone – we do it for *pleasure to keep us fit.*" Ensured Alicia.

"What an upside-down world you live in! I'm glad I will never see it." Said Albert, still shaking his head.

With that, the dusty, hard-working couple returned to their task. It wasn't too long before once again the two of them were finished, and Toby was pulling them back down the *Leeds and Liverpool Canal* to *Leeds Centre,* and mooring near *Leeds Bridge.*

"Jamie won't have such a long walk when he finished work." Observed Alicia.

"No lass, he'll be back soon!"

"I've been thinking, Albert – after seeing me work with you this week, are you more encouraged to let Alice have a go?"

"Do you mean *doing John's work*?"

"Yes! I think she would love it – and you won't be short-handed when John is working and bringing in a wage."

"I don't think it has *ever been done…what will people say?"* said Albert.

"They all think *I'm Alice* – and nobody has batted an eyelid!"

"You're right there, lass – if Alice is up for it, I'll give it a go. Mind I'll be left high and dry if she finds a suitor!"

Alicia thought for a moment, then said, "That won't happen. I don't know *why* I say that…but it won't."

"Maybe the young *Freddie Chambers* will be the only one she'll meet…because to be honest, apart from saying she wants to meet a gentleman, it's never gone any further than that! And there won't be much chance of *finding* a gentleman looking like you do now, will there?"

Alicia looked down at her coal-dust-covered dress and said, "You're right there, Albert."

A Switch in Time

She looked all around and saw there was nobody about. Seeing the coast was clear, she pulled her dress off over her head, taking with it her long vest, and gave both garments a vigorous shaking, removing the dust. She hadn't given a *thought* to the fact she was standing there *quite naked in front of Albert*, but when she turned towards him, he was busying himself shaping some wood with his pen-knife without a care for her nakedness. Alicia replaced her clothes and went over to Albert, kissing him on his cheek. This brought a smile to his face, and he asked, "What was that for?"

"For *being who you are*. The men from my time could learn *much* from you, Albert – you are a truly *great man*."

"Well, lass, I don't know about that, but thank you anyway!" said Albert, his rough cheeks showing a bit of a flush.

Time was passing by for Jamie at work as he was watching a piston being fitted to a cylinder. He was making notes of *everything he was seeing* – but not letting anyone *see him doing it*. As soon as he had filled his own notebook with relevant information, it was going into the wall with the rest of his treasure. The notebook for John was coming along nicely, too. Jamie was in his *element* in this environment, and was sure John would take to it too. The engineer liked him, the foreman liked him, and the troublesome young workers would leave him alone for sure. *Everything was beginning to add up – and the only fly in the ointment, so to speak, was Freddie Chambers – why had his name cropped up?* A steam horn blasted outside, signifying the end of the working day, and Jamie was wondering what Doris had made for supper. He rushed out of the factory and down to the canal, where to his surprise, Toby was there munching on his nosebag.

"Hello, you two!" said Jamie happily when he saw Albert and Alicia.

Alicia ran to him and gave him the love.

"I'm forever in *your debt* Albert, for what you have done for my sister…"

"The debt *is paid* for what you have done for my John." Albert answered.

The warming glow of fire and candlelight escaped from the cabin. With it came a waft of Doris' stew.

"Come and get it, you lot!" said Doris.

Like a flash, all three of them were downstairs, enjoying Doris's simple but beautiful stew.

In the 21st century, night had also drawn in, and John Watson had had the *best day of his life*. He had spent the day looking at engines from the 1810 period to the 1870s, and showed *no interest to any of the locomotives* that most had come to see. After his day with John, Bob Jones said, "I have to say, John, you have been the *most interested person* I have *ever shown* these types of locomotives to. You've also been the *strangest* – not wanting to see the *Mallard,* the *Flying Scotsman* or the *Royal Coaches!*"

"What are they?" asked John.

"What do you *mean?* These are the *most famous* railway-related items *in the world!"* exclaimed Bob.

"But I have never heard of them…I'm sorry…"

Bob Jones once again just scratched his head, and said, "Did you get all the information you needed on the least-known locos that you wanted?"

"I have sir – but you are *wrong about these engines* – their fame has even reached us on the *canal*. I was only talking to my father about that very thing a few days ago! You *mark my words Mr. Jones – these things will take over the canals, because they can deliver things MUCH QUICKER.*"

A Switch in Time

"I'm sure you're right." Said Bob Jones, hardly believing his own ears. "Well then, let's take you back to the entrance to meet Freddie and your sister."

Freddie and Alice were on their way back, enjoying another romantic ride in a beautiful horse-drawn coach. Alice's day had been *perfect*. The shops, the meal – and for the *first time in her life*, visiting *York* in all its splendour.

"I have had the *best time ever!* Thank you so much!" said Alice.

"I have too. Look – there's John with Bob!"

As the chestnut-coloured mare was brought to a halt outside the National Railway Museum, Freddie said, "Hop in, John."

Looking at Bob's puzzled face, he continued, "Is everything okay, Bob?"

"Everything was fine. I'm over in Leeds in a few days – I'll call in and see you and Jamie, to see how the *world's greatest railway* is coming along."

"I shall look forward to it – and thank you for today!"

With that, the driver tapped the horse with the reigns and said, "Where to now, sir?"

"The *station*, please – I think I have two *very tired people here*."

In the short distance from the National Railway Museum to York Railway Station, the two Victorian siblings fell fast asleep.

Back in time on the canal, supper was over and the pots were all washed and put away. This was the time Alicia had begun to love most – the family all together around the fire, talking about their day. Usually it was Albert who started the proceedings, but this time it was Jamie, telling everyone about his great discovery. Everyone listened intently as he told them about the mouldings under the floor and the bricked-up furnace.

"Why have they bricked up the furnace?" Asked Albert.

"It seems they couldn't get the iron right; so rather than dismantle it, they bricked it up to preserve it, until someone came up with an answer. But then they found it was cheaper to have it done elsewhere. Now – I have been making notes for *John* – it's very simple instructions for what I have been doing this week, so he knows who is who when he gets here. Alf Wheelwright will be able to *read them to him*."

"Right then, lad! Let me tell you *my news* – your *sister did the barge almost single-handedly today – in fact, the only thing she DIDN'T do was tend to Toby!*" enthused Albert.

Everyone in the cabin began to clap, so Alicia stood up and gave them a theatrical curtsey. "Why, thank you all!" she said. The loudest and the longest applause came from her *very proud brother*.

"Oh, well done, Alicia! Let me give you a hug!"

The two siblings hugged each other tightly. Alicia was proud of her achievement – but her heart swelled at the *love* she was feeling from her brother. Jamie smiled and gave his sister a kiss on the cheek, whispering in her ear, "Dad would be *so proud of you right now*...I do hope this isn't *all a dream*..."

Alicia squeezed his hand and said, "This is as *real as it gets – I will be like this FROM NOW ON...*"

Jamie hugged her once more, much to the joy of Albert and Doris.

Albert reached for his little squeezebox, and once again the sounds of laughter and singing could be heard from the hard-working barge family.

Sunday dawned over the canal, and a day of rest for this particular week.

"What happens on a Sunday?" asked Alicia.

"A day off, I reckon!" announced Albert.

A Switch in Time

"Good! I can catch up on my sewing! If anyone needs anything patching, let me have it…" said Doris.

"You can take Toby into the field, so he can kick up his legs." Albert instructed young James.

"No – let me…" said Alicia, "I would love to do that!"

"That will mean James will just *idle the day away doing nothing of importance!*" Said Doris.

"It's called *playing*…" said Alicia with a smile and a wink for young James.

"Woohooooo!" shrieked James, as he flashed past everyone and skipped off the boat.

"*Playing indeed, at his age – you'll be making him SOFT…*" observed Albert.

Alicia stood up, kissed Albert and Doris, waved at Jamie and then went to find Toby.

"What are *you* doing, lad?" asked Albert.

"I am *going to fulfil a dream, Albert, and take a walk around the Victorian Centre of Leeds…*" said Jamie.

Placing his flat cap on his head, he bid Albert and Doris a good day and embarked upon his adventure.

Alicia had led Toby to an open field, and let him off to run. Although Toby did not have a saddle, and she was *definitely* not dressed for riding, only having her dressing coat on with no undergarments, she was determined to still try to ride *Lightning's* magnificent horse. She made a clicking sound with her mouth, and Toby's ears twisted in her direction. He then trotted over to where she stood. She stroked his face, and remembered how *lovingly beautiful these animals were.* Toby gave a slight whinny as Alicia grasped his mane, and then she kicked her leg up high and jumped at the same time, straddling the horse. As her naked bottom landed on Toby's back, a cold shudder engulfed her. As

John Paul Bernett

her bum and the horse's back warmed to each other, both horse and rider relaxed. The *slightest tap of her heel*, and Toby began to trot. Under the old way of thinking, this animal and this girl would not have even *been in the same field* – also, Alicia would be wearing *thousands of pounds worth of designer riding clothes*. The *very thought that her pampered rear being in contact with the thoroughbred horse beneath her* – *never mind an OLD NAG* – *would have been ABSURD.* She giggled to herself, as she now experienced *bareback riding* – in *every sense of the word* – and had discovered it was *pure FUN*. Her mind was full of what her old friends would think of her now. She was very giddy…and had it been summer and not winter, and would have probably discarded what was indeed her *entire wardrobe* on the ground as she rode. There were parts of Alicia that she was discovering and *loving* – she had spent a lot of her time in the 19th century actually *enjoying herself* – and for the *life of her, she couldn't remember the last time she was this happy…*

The first impressions of Victorian Leeds were that all the stone buildings were as black as coal. As Jamie walked along *The Calls*, he made his way to *Leeds Bridge*, and stood there taking in the sights. Horse-drawn carriages, elegantly-dressed ladies and gentlemen, and tradesmen and young urchins could be seen in every direction. This was the *first chance to view the bridge as it was before its rebuild.* YES! This was *excitement indeed* to the history graduate. As it had been all through this week and the 19th century, he spent a lot of his time coughing. 21st century lungs had long since not had to deal with coal smoke, dust and smog, but that was a small price to pay for Jamie. He turned right and wandered up what he knew as *Lower Briggate* – and instead of a bridge going across, it was just a street, with shops on either side. There was a throng of shoppers – even though it was Sunday – with shop-keepers shouting out their wares. Horses, carriages, and children seemed to make it all sound even louder than it was in his time…how could that be, without the buses, cars and motorbikes? Then he realized…all around there was the sound of *steam engines*…he had heard it all the way

A Switch in Time

down the canal, and could still hear it on *Lower Briggate* – but he just couldn't get used to it without the bridge across. He knew the Leeds Viaduct wasn't built until 1869, and all the steam locomotives would stop at Marsh Lane Station. He continued up Briggate, marvelling at the old buildings – most of which had been *long gone* in the 21st century. Tudor buildings with their black *Jacobean Oak,* and little shops and lending houses lined both sides of the poorly-maintained road. *Oh, this was a different Leeds indeed…and Jamie was LOVING EVERY MINUTE OF IT.*

Down the canal, his sister was walking up the towpath, holding onto Toby's reins. She was sporting a thoughtful expression. She had decided that the name *Alicia* didn't befit her new outlook on life…and *Alice* was *such a beautiful name.*

On arriving back at the barge, she announced her decision to Albert and Doris.

"Well, you *certainly aren't that horrible young person that arrived here last week, young lady, I can TELL YOU THAT!*" said Albert.

"Thank GOD!" replied Alicia.

"C'mere, my girl." Said Doris, taking a cloth from her apron pocket, pushing her finger into the cloth and licking the tip of it. She took hold of Alicia's chin and wiped away a spot of dirt from her cheek. This basic act of loving care made Alicia think of her *mother* again, and *how pathetic she had been as a parent.* Once her face was spot-free, she enquired, "Anyone for tea?"

"Always ready for one of those, lass!" agreed Albert.

Alicia took the teapot, put a little water in it, swished it around and then threw the old tea leaves into the canal. Showing she had been watching Doris, she put a little boiling water in the teapot and swirled it around again to warm the pot. She then proceeded to make the tea – just in time for Jamie's return – and the whole family settled in the twilight for another evening of family talking. The talk, of course, was about horse riding – and *steam engines.* Poor old Doris couldn't even get a word in.

An uneventful Sunday in the 21st century was also drawing to a close. John and Alice had spent the day still recovering from the trip to York, and *John in particular,* from his last few days at Armley Mills continuing his training – although his trainer had no real idea that that was what he was doing. He just thought he had a very enthusiastic young man. So, their Sunday had consisted of *lounging about on couches*, talking about John's experiences in the mills, and at York. Freddie and Alice had spent most of the time arm-in-arm on the couch listening. Alice, although very tired herself, went to her younger brother and took his shoes off to make him comfortable. Freddie in the meantime was making a beverage in the kitchen, when Alice walked in and said, "Freddie Chambers?"

"Yes...?" he replied, looking slightly confused.

"I *remember*!"

"You *remember what?*"

"*I have heard your sweet name before!*" said a serious Alice.

"How could you have *possibly heard MY name, Alice?*"

"A very distant memory..." answered Alice, as she reached up to give him a kiss on the cheek.

"Do you...want to talk about it?" he asked.

"There's nothing much to tell...only...I *know our paths have crossed before...*"

"Do you mean you have known someone with the *same name as me?*"

"I can't remember..." she said, shaking her head, "But something tells me *it was YOU.*"

"If that is the case, then we will *definitely meet again.*" Said Freddie with a reassuring smile.

"Yes…we *will*. There will be *nobody else for me when I get back*…for I *now believe…I have already met you in my time – but that's okay, for we will meet again…and again…*" she said with a yawn.

"C'mon, sleepy, let's go to bed." Said Freddie.

CHAPTER 19

Monday dawned in the 19th and 21st centuries. As Freddie Chambers, Alice Watson and John Watson slept in their beds, Albert and Doris Watson, Alicia Winters and young James – and of course, Toby the horse, were making their way back to *Thwaite Gate* to pick up a new load of coal. Jamie Winters was starting what was to be his *last day*, as *John Winters, apprentice to the engineer*. Jamie was whistling *'A Forest'*, by The Cure, as he arrived at work. He quickly removed his coat and accepted a mug of steaming tea that was almost instantly delivered to him. As the strong, hot beverage began to warm him up, the engineer, back earlier than expected, shouted for him to go to the office.

"John, my boy – how are things going?"

"Very well, sir." Answered Jamie.

"Tomorrow is *Tuesday*...and a *new locomotive is coming to the station*...and I want YOU to see it. So, I want you to meet me there at ten a.m."

"Do you want me to come here first?" asked Jamie.

"No – I don't want you full of oil and grime – just come straight to Marsh Lane."

"I will look forward to that, Sir!" said Jamie.

The first realization then came to his mind that tomorrow might be *the day of the switch*. It would be *one week exactly...and all of a sudden, it was going to be a day he DIDN'T HAVE TO WORK*. He began to wonder if all he had learned in his week in the past would stay in his consciousness. He began to think up *another plan...he would write down EVERY SINGLE THING,* up to the

A Switch in Time

end of his work today, and hide the book in the cellar with the other goodies from the past.

As Albert toked on his pipe, Alicia's grip on the tiller as her train of thought changed.

"Penny for 'em, lass…" said Albert.

"I'm wondering what lies ahead…" she answered.

"*Good things lass – and plenty of them!*"

"I hope so, Albert, I *really do*…"

"Maybe your first port of call should be *your father*…"

"*Ohh….there are SO MANY I HAVE WRONGED, ALBERT*…and it's weighing heavy on my mind."

"That RIGHT THERE tells you that you are a *better person*."

"How so?"

"Before, you had *nothing that weighed heavy* – because you didn't care for anybody but yourself." He answered. He stood up and announced, "We are here!"

Alicia steered the barge to the towpath and handed the tiller to Albert, just in time to stop Doris coming up from below.

"I will tie the boat off, Doris." Offered Alicia with a smile.

"Are you sure lass?" asked Doris.

"Yes!" shouted Alicia, as she jumped over the side, taking with her the stern rope. Like before, she quickly tied it off and ran to the bow. Doris had made her way there and threw the bow rope to Alicia. Catching it the first time, she wrapped it around the post and drew the bow to the canal side.

Back in Holbeck, Jamie was cleaning his bosses' office as the engineer checked the drawings of his latest designs.

"Come over and look at these drawings with me, John...and tell me what you think it is."

Jamie put his sweeping brush down and moved quickly to the drawing board. Looking at the drawing, he knew *exactly what it was*, but realizing he was in the guise of John Watson, he said, "Is it a *steam engine,* Sir?"

"It's a *steam locomotive*...you will have to learn the difference. In my view, a steam engine is a *static engine that powers machines, like the one in our factory.* A *locomotive is a LIVING THING that RUNS ON RAILS...AND IS THE FUTURE OF TRANSPORTATION...*"

"We certainly live in exciting times, Sir!" observed Jamie.

"Indeed we do, boy, *Indeed we do...*"

The two men spent the next hour going over the simplest parts of a steam locomotive, and Jamie was in his element. This was not because of what he was *learning*, because he *already knew what he was being taught. He already knew what the engineer was telling him...he also knew MORE than the engineer's restricted view of steam power – but it was such an IMMENSE PRIVELEDGE to be in the room with such a PIONEER.* Again, Jamie hoped that this feeling would stay with him when he journeyed back to his own time.

In 2013, Monday had arrived as well. John Watson had already been picked up by Lee Coates, and was hard at work in the museum cleaning the locomotive that had been run over the weekend. Lee called him into his office.

"Sit down, John...I would like a word with you."

John sat, somewhat uneasily, in the office chair.

"Have I done *something wrong?*"

A Switch in Time

"No, John! Not at all! I just wanted to say that I am *very impressed* with what you have learned this week. You are certainly a very good student."

John looked at him and said, "Student? I...I don't know what you mean..."

"You don't know what a *student* is?"

"No sir, I don't..." answered John.

"Never mind – it's not important. Can I ask you a question, John?"

"*Anything.*" Was John's reply.

"I know you are living with Freddie Chambers at the moment...but *where do you live normally?*"

"I live on board my father's canal barge."

"I see – *what canal do you moor?*"

"Mostly the *Calder Navigation* – not far from Thwaite Gate – or the *Leeds/Liverpool* – why do you ask?"

"Because I'm thinking of setting you on *permanently.*"

John's eyes *widened* at the thought of *finally working with steam engines.*

"So...about this *barge you live on*...how many berths is it?"

"I don't understand your question." Answered John.

"Yaknow...how many bedrooms?"

John began to laugh, and said, "There are no bedrooms *on a canal barge – EVERYBODY knows that!*"

"These are just *aptitude questions,* John – it's a way of me finding out how smart you are – so just answer, even if the question seems *silly.*"

John nodded his head, having totally forgotten about his situation.

"Next question, John. Who is the current Monarch?"

Again, John looked bewildered by the question.

"Who is the King or Queen, John?"

"That's *easy – Queen Victoria*!" was the instant reply.

Without flinching, Lee asked another question. "What cargo do you *transport on your barge*?"

"Coal! The most *powerful fuel in the WORLD*!"

"Last question, John. What is the name of your horse?"

"Toby! He is a fine, strong horse!" he replied without a thought of what he was saying.

Lee Coates looked at John and said, "That's fine, John. Now, why don't you go to the café and get yourself some dinner."

As soon as John left his office, Lee Coates rang Freddie Chambers' phone.

"Hello, Lee! There is nothing *wrong, is there?*"

"I want to know *what's going on.*"

"What do you mean?"

"*John Watson. There is something you're not telling me.* I was talking to Bob Jones from York this morning. I asked him what he thought of our friend John…he told me he was the *strangest guy he had ever shown around.* For instance – he was the ONLY LOCOMOTIVE ENTHUSIAST that has never heard of the 'Flying Scotsman' or the 'Mallard'…and he was only interested in the Rocket…in a conversation just now, he told me the NAME OF THE CURRENT MONARCH IS VICTORIA…"

"Um…well…like I was saying, he lives in a…"

"COAL BARGE. Not a Mennonite society!"

"Um…uhh…I don't know what to say…" Freddie answered nervously.

"You have had him with me, surrounded by Victorian machinery – he *doesn't understand* modern swear words! He informed me that *canal barges do not have bedrooms, and the one he lives on HAULS COAL,* AND IS POWERED BY A HORSE NAMED TOBY!!"

"We need to talk…but not like this. I will come and see you tomorrow sometime. I won't be in when you drop John off tonight."

"Tomorrow it is, then."

With that, they both ended the phone call. Freddie took a sharp intake of breath and turned towards the bedroom. At the door stood a worried-looking Alice.

"What's the matter, Freddie?"

"That was Lee Coates."

"I didn't see him…"

"What?" said Freddie in frustration…then quickly realizing he had never used his phone in front of the siblings before. "It's just a little machine that lets people talk to each other – with it, the person you want to talk to doesn't need to be with you."

"It doesn't look like you liked what he had to say…" said Alice, not really understanding.

"Well, Alice, you're right – John let something *slip* today…"

"He wasn't *hurt*, was he?"

"Hurt? Oh, no no…Alice, it's just a saying – what I mean is…he told Lee some things about you two that I wish he hadn't."

"Let's not spoil the day with something my silly brother has done…" offered Alice with a smile.

"You are right, my love…we may have precious little time left…"

Alice held out her hand and Freddie took hold of it, placing his other arm around his beloved's waist. He pulled her towards himself and kissed her eager mouth.

As it was now midday, Freddie decided to take Alice for a treat. With exception of the burger she had had at Kirkstall Abbey, everything she'd eaten had been what she could eat in her own time. Freddie deemed that today would be different – they would eat Thai cuisine! They both donned their winter coats and made their way out into the cold but bright day.

"Where are we going, Freddie?"

"To one of my favourite *Thai restaurants.*"

"Well why are we in the market, then?"

"Because here it is…"

The two of them stopped at a small Thai café at the bottom of the market called 'May's Thai Café'. There were only three tables outside, and two small ones within – but it served the *best Thai food in Leeds,* in Freddie's humble opinion. As they sat down, the resonance of May's laughter could be heard from inside. It was the kind of laughter that made you smile, *whatever your mood.* A distinguished gentleman came out to take their order. Raj was his name – a multilingual, educated man who did the 'front of house' for his lovely wife May. He *always* greeted Freddie with a smile, and Freddie introduced him to Alice, saying, "This is my *new wife, Alice*…Alice, this is my good friend Raj."

From inside, May had overheard the conversation and made a rare trip away from her many woks to come and say hi.

"Will it be drunken rice for you, Freddie?" asked Raj, knowing his favourite.

"Yes, please. Alice has never eaten Thai before and has *never had anything with chillies.*"

"In that case, may I suggest *Pad Thai Gai*? It has no chillies…"

Alice eagerly nodded her head.

The food soon arrived and Alice just looked at it in *amazement. Never before had she seen such colour and beauty in a bowl of food.*

"Those are called *noodles,* Alice…and the meat is chicken."

Alice took a tentative first morsel of food. As she began to chew, her taste buds sprang to life and her eyes opened wide.

"I have *never tasted anything like this in my life!*" she exclaimed, eagerly placing another forkful into her delicate mouth.

"I'm so glad you like it." Smiled Freddie.

When the wonderful lunch was over, Freddie and Alice bid Raj and May goodbye, and were exploring the *market* in Leeds. Again, Alice ran from stall to stall like an excited little girl. Freddie just smiled – and tried to keep up with her.

The afternoon wore on, and the winter daylight began to fade into grey-blue, and then the black of night. Somehow, Freddie knew…*that with the sun…his time with Alice had waned, too.*

At Armley Mills, John had finished his task and was waiting on Lee Coates, who was finishing some paperwork. John looked about the place – as if for the last time. He didn't know *why* he thought that…it just felt that way. Lee exited his office and locked the door.

"C'mon, John, stop your daydreaming and let's get you home."

"Okay." Said John, as he gingerly opened the car door and carefully stepped inside.

The drive home was again uneventful for Lee…but a ride of *torture* for the Victorian. John had, in fact, kept his eyes closed for the entire journey again. As they pulled up into *The Calls*, John was first out of the car and went round to where Lee was sitting.

"Thank you for all you have learned me." He said, smiling at Lee with gratefulness.

"For all I have *taught* you." Corrected Lee.

John just looked confused and shook Lee's hand.

"Will I see you again?" asked Lee.

John thought for a second, but looked even *more confused* and said, "Yes...umm...no...uhh...tomorrow? I don't know."

Lee just smiled and shook his head, saying, "Tell Freddie not to forget about tomorrow."

"I will tell him." Answered John as he walked away towards what had been his home for the last week.

Lee drove off, and as he did, John heard a voice calling him from behind. It was Freddie and Alice, arriving back from the town centre. The three of them went inside and up to the penthouse. Once inside, Freddie asked John what had happened today, and John replied that he had taken an 'aptitude' test – and that he had done well with it. Freddie of course instantly realized what Lee had done...and wondered how he was going to *explain all of this, now his Mennonite theory was totally out of the window.*

The evening was spent talking about all of the wonderful things both of the siblings had experienced during their week, and how *big* and *noisy* Leeds had become. Freddie realized that although they had spoken about going back to their time, the two siblings had forgotten that it was *imminent.* With that in mind, Freddie carried on with all the talk about what a wonderful time they were having. The chatting went on until bedtime. Freddie and Alice bid John farewell and went to their bed, whilst John settled down on the comfy couch.

A Switch in Time

On the other side of the canal – *and time* – night had also fallen. Teatime was over and the pots washed. The galley had been turned back into a makeshift bedroom, and all the family were sitting around the stove talking.

"My ideas about what a lasses' work is have *changed. You have shown me how STRONG a woman can be – and my outlook in general about things has changed, young Alice."* Said Albert.

"Thank you, Albert! I've never changed anyone's mind for them before in my life!" Alicia answered honestly.

"You have gone up in my estimations 100%!" offered Jamie. "Are you going to let Alice help you on the barge...and let John build his future in Engineering, Albert? He continued.

"Aye lad! If that is what they both want, it is *fine by me.*"

"Having a son who is an engineer will help when Toby is eventually *replaced with a steam engine.*" Remarked Jamie.

"I'm not sure about that, lad! It would take up *too much room – and I wouldn't be able to carry enough coal*!"

"The thing is – when you are *motorized* – you will be able to pull *several boats behind you...and you will be able to transport up to TEN TIMES MORE COAL per journey than you do now!*" informed Jamie.

Albert scratched his chin and looked deep in thought. The idea pleased him greatly. He remembered his friend *Tom* talking about such things.

"What about unloading?" asked Albert.

"Don't worry yourself about *unloading*, Albert, steam will change that too! You mustn't fight the changes, for *they are coming*. Many of your contemporaries will be left *behind...but you WON'T. BECAUSE YOU WILL BE FORWARD-THINKING. YOU WILL HAVE A SON WHO WILL BE ABLE TO EXPLAIN THE NEW TECHNOLOGY TO YOU...AND YOU WILL BE THE ONLY MAN*

WITH THE SENSE TO LET YOUR DAUGHTER WORK ALONGSIDE YOU!"

"It all sounds a bit scary to me…but I will do my *best*." Answered Albert.

"We know you DO – we have seen the result of how your business *has grown…*" said Alicia.

Albert stood up and announced, "There will be *no work tomorrow – so we get all this off to the right start, I will be putting all that painting skill you talked about young Alicia to good use – and we will DO A NEW SIGN, TO MARK OUR NEW BEGINNING.*"

"Well then! If there are going to be so many new changes tomorrow, we'd better get an early night!" said Doris.

The candles were blown out on the little coal barge in the 19th century, and the entire crew all drifted peacefully to sleep.

A Switch in Time

CHAPTER 15

Tuesday dawned a bright and sunny morning in both the 21st and the 19th centuries. Albert had already gotten the paint ready for Alicia. Doris was washing the morning pots. Jamie had an appointment to meet his boss at the train station in two hours' time, and Alicia was *ready – paint brush in hand – to BEGIN.*

"Okay, Albert…what do you want me to paint on the sign?" she asked.

"I want to be able to *remember the both of you when you return to your own time, so this is what I want you to paint:* ALBERT WINTERS AND DAUGHTER."

"Are you sure, Albert?" queried a puzzled Alicia.

"I don't think I've *ever been as sure of anything in my LIFE!*" Albert answered.

Alicia took as much care painting Albert's new sign as she used to when she was painting her own nails, and the end result was *stunning. It looked like it had been painted by a sign-writer.* Albert stood on the towpath and looked at his new sign – and he was indeed a *happy man.*

"Now THAT is a GOOD JOB, lass…I couldn't have done better myself!"

"Thank you, sir!" said Alicia, taking a bow.

Jamie came up from the galley and jumped onto the towpath. Looking a bit bemused by the surname on the boat, but somehow knowing it was *right,* he said, "Great work, sis! And an early blow for the *Suffragette Movement*! Do you fancy taking a walk to the station with me?"

"Sure!" answered Alice.

"Be careful, you two – there's a nasty-looking storm coming…" Albert observed.

The two siblings looked towards Leeds, and sure enough, there was a strange cloud formation building up in front of them. Alicia and Jamie stared at each other…realizing that they had seen this before. Albert cautioned them both.

"I don't like the look of those clouds, John! Don't be more than an hour with your *magic lanterns*…" Albert muttered.

Again, Jamie and Alicia looked at each other with puzzled expressions, and Jamie shouted back, "We will be back before you know it, dad."

Turning back to his sister, he said, "*It's happening again, sis – and Albert is starting to FORGET – he thinks we are JOHN AND ALICE, SETTING OFF A WEEK AGO!*"

John began to run towards the cloud formation, still holding onto Alicia's hand.

"C'mon sis…it's time *to go home."*

The two ran as fast as their legs could carry them, and it wasn't long before they reached the place where they originally landed a week ago.

"Look, Jamie! The cloud is above us!" shouted Alicia.

Wind was now whistling in their eyes…lightning flashes were all around them. Jamie felt his feet lift off of the ground as they both began to float upwards.

In the 21st century, Freddie told John Watson that he had to pop out for a few minutes because there was *something that he had to sort out at the bank.* He grabbed his jacket and picked up an envelope, saying, "Alice will be out in a minute – she's just finishing dressing."

With that, he was off on his financial business.

Alice came into the room fastening her blouse and saw John staring out of the window.

"What are you looking at?" she asked.

"It's a strange cloud in the sky – come and see!"

John opened the balcony doors as his sister joined him. They both stepped out onto the balcony, and Alice let out a scream as the cloud *engulfed them.*

"Freddie!!"

Again, John and Alice realized they were *not alone in the vortex.* As they were realizing this, so were Jamie and Alicia, and the two pairs of siblings passed by each other again. Seconds later, John and Alice were on the towpath – and Jamie and Alicia stood on the balcony, and both pairs of them *were on the right side of time.*

The vortex disappeared leaving the two in an awkward silence, and then Alicia said softly, "From here on in, I want to be called *Alice.*"

Her brother smiled, and threw his arms around her, squeezingher tightly.

On the other side of the canal, John and Alice found themselves sitting on the ground in their old clothes. They both looked at each other, and John said, "We are back *home.*"

Alice looked at him with tears in her eyes, and whispered, "*I didn't get to say goodbye to Freddie…*"

A Switch in Time

"That's a *good thing* – we have our lives to live in the *here and now*…and you are HERE. You will be seeing him again…of this I have *no doubt.*"

"He will *always be in my heart…and there we will be together FOREVER.*" And then another thought came into her mind – the thought of her MOM and DAD. At the top of her voice, she shouted, "Mom and dad! C'mon John, *let's GO HOME!*"

"You go home sis…I'm going to the train station."

"Why?"

"I…I'm *not quite sure…but something tells me I will find out there.*"

"Okay, John, I'm going home…I will see you there."

With those words, John walked off towards the train station, and Alice shot down the canal side as fast as her tiny feet could carry her. As she arrived at the barge, the first member of the family she saw was *Toby* – whose ears flicked forward when he saw her. She wrapped her arms around his mane and kissed him on the side of his head. Toby whinnied with approval. She then ran to the stern of the barge, shouting, "Mother!"

At this point, she stopped *dead on her feet*, as she caught sight of the new sign. Albert appeared on deck with outstretched arms and the *widest of all smiles on his face.*

"Dad!" screamed Alice, as she buried her slight self into his loving arms. "We are *back, dad! We have been in the FUTURE! I've missed you so much! What does the new sign mean? Where's mom?*"

Albert laughed heartily. "One question at a time, lass…" he said with a smile. "While you were gone for your *look around Leeds*, your mother and I *made some changes. How do you feel about taking your brother's place and getting more involved in the running of the barge?*"

"Dad – I would *love* that!"

"But, what if you find this *gentleman* you were so keen on finding?"

"I'm not looking anymore, dad – my life is *fulfilled,* and I am happy to stay *as I am.*"

"Well, that's settled then, lass – you are now my partner! Your brother will be learning to become an *engineer*...has he gone to the station?"

"*Yes...how did you know that?*"

"*I just did.*" Was Albert's reply.

At this point in the conversation, Doris had come up from below. She grabbed Alice and gave her a big squeeze.

"Hello, Alice, my little angel!"

"Hello mom! I've missed you *so much!*"

"We have missed you too, Alice...now, come below, and tell me all about it while I put the kettle on."

Albert took a large toke on his pipe and felt somewhat relieved that his daughter and son were *back.* Though his memories of the previous week were beginning to fade – as if in a *dream – he knew his new sign would keep him moving towards a destiny that had been set up for him by RELATIVES FROM THE FUTURE.* One thought that would never fade was, '*Don't fight the future – accept it with open arms, and pull coal boats BEHIND YOU.*'

Once Doris and Alice were comfortable downstairs, mother asked daughter about the previous week.

"It was all clear in my head a minute or two ago...but it's *fading...and there is a lot I cannot seem to remember – but one thing I will never forget is Freddie Chambers...*"

"Do you mean that tall boy you used to play with as a child?" asked Doris.

"In a way I think I do – but it would be hard for you to understand. But, like I told my dad, I am *no longer looking for a man in this life, because as a woman, I am now fulfilled...*" she said with a small tear in her eye.

Doris just put her arms around her once more, as the memory of Alicia faded *fully away from her mind...and thoughts of Alice never having left replaced it.*

"There is one thing though, mom – my *tummy feels strange – it is as though Freddie is still with me...does that sound silly?*"

Doris looked at Alice, and lifted her face by gently raising her chin with her hand. "You said you were a *fulfilled woman – I think in a few months, Albert will have his GRANDCHILD he was so looking forward to...*"

Alice's eyes widened fully as she put her hands over her mouth, and whispered, "*Do you mean...a baby?*"

Doris smiled and nodded her head. Alice danced around the little room hand in hand with her smiling mother. An out-of-breath Doris then said, "That's enough dancing Alice! Your father will be wondering where his pot of tea is!"

Alice took her father his mug of tea. Her memory of the past week fading with every step she took. By the time she had reached her father, all that was left was *Freddie Chambers...and the knowledge that his baby was growing inside of her...and that one day they would reunite.*

Along the towpath, a woman came walking down holding a baby. As she reached the boat, she stopped and looked at Alice. She beckoned Alice towards her. She then took hold of Alice's hand and said, "*I was given this ring by an angel...and my fortune has changed! I want to pass it on to YOU...I don't want you to ask why...it's the only thing that I can do for you. Please accept it. I hope it will help you like it helped me.*"

Alice said, "Thank you." And placed the ring on her finger. She said to the woman, "I will keep it *forever...*"

With that, the woman smiled, and went on her way, *never to be seen again.*

John by now had arrived at the station, and walked up to a well-dressed man. Taking his flat-cap off he said, "I am here, sir!"

"Indeed you are, my young apprentice! I have just arrived myself! And so has what I have brought you here to see..."

Both men walked up to the track, and there stood *one of the latest steam locomotives to arrive in Leeds from the Stephenson's Works in the Northeast.*

"Now what do you think of THAT, lad?" asked the engineer.

"I have *never seen the like of it, Sir! Will WE be building this type of locomotive?*"

"This is for passenger trains...the type of locomotive I design are for *industry – for moving coal and iron ore around...*"

"I see...do you think *canal barges* will ever have engines, Sir?"

"Undoubtedly, my curious fellow – but only by the *forward-thinking canal boat owners. The rest, I'm afraid, will not be able to compete with the railway as it grows...*"

"One day, I will build a steam engine small enough to fit in my dad's boat!"

"An ambitious statement! One that you will have to do a *full five-year apprenticeship with ME to fulfill!*"

"It's something I am *greatly looking forward to, Sir...*"

"EXCELLENT! This country rules the world with engineering! And if we are going to stay that way, we need *hungry young men like YOU taking part in the game*! By the way – I noticed this morning at the office...I seem not to have taken note of your surname..."

A Switch in Time

"Winters, Sir...my name is *John Winters*."

His mind was *racing...full of everything Freddie Chambers, Lee Coates and Bob Jones had taught him.* Also fixed firmly in his mind was everything that Jamie had learned in his stead. John Winters was a 19th century surfer on the crest of an industrial wave...and he LOVED IT. He had seen a glimpse into the future – and now it was time to MAKE THAT FUTURE HAPPEN.

After close inspection of the new locomotive, the two men went back to the factory, and John's apprenticeship began. After what had seemed a very long day, his first day at work was finally over and he returned to the barge.

"Now then, lad – did you have a good day at work?" enquired Albert.

"Yes, dad – another good day."

"So...you have your *first week behind you...well done!*"

"Thank you, dad."

"Well Alice, how was your first week working properly on the barge?" asked John.

"It was *easy*...I did it *a lot better than YOU did!*" she said, sticking out her tongue.

"Oh you did, did you? Well, I can tell you this...you didn't get *dirty enough! C'mere!*" he said, rubbing his hands in the coals chasing after her, first onto the deck, and then down the towpath with his arms outstretched and his sister screaming and running away.

CHAPTER 16

Alicia, holding Jamie's hand, stepped into the penthouse, and she could not *believe* the size of it. With a hearty laugh, she said, "All this space for *one person!*" She then looked at her finger...and there was *the ring she gave the little woman in rags with the baby.* She began to cry.

"C'mon, sis – it's okay...do you remember everything that took place over the last week?"

"Every *last detail...and the memory is getting STRONGER AND STRONGER in my mind!*" she sobbed.

"Good! So have I! I need to get to my place *as soon as possible!*"

"You go, Jamie...I have an *awful lot to think about.* I will be fine." She said, kissing him on his cheek, and then they both departed.

In his excitement, Jamie didn't wait for the elevator – he ran straight down the stairs. He burst out of the door and straight into Freddie Chambers, knocking him over and sending papers flying everywhere.

"Freddie!" shouted Jamie. "Just the man I wanted to see! C'mon, we have *work to do!*"

"WHAT? *Jamie? You're back! Hello mate! Have I got some news for you! There is someone I want you to meet – come on, she's upstairs!*"

"There is no-one upstairs, Freddie, except for *Alicia.* Who is it that you want me to meet?"

A Switch in Time

The impact of his friend being back in this century suddenly hit Freddie.

"So...if you two are back here...I guess John and Alice are back in the 19th century..."

"Safe and sound, and back in their own time!" affirmed Jamie.

Freddie hung his head and said, *"Nobody – I have just remembered. You probably know of them already.* So what's *so important* that we have to go *right now*?"

"Come on and I'll *show you!"* replied Jamie, grabbing Freddie by his shoulders. "I'm *so glad to see you again!*"

Once in the car, Jamie looked at Freddie and reiterated, "It's great to see you, pal! What a week I have had! If you have followed my instructions, I suppose *your week would have been quite boring and kind of weird!*"

"Weird is *one way* to describe it...educational is another...but WONDROUS is perhaps the *best way* of describing it. I don't suppose you got the chance to leave the *'Wicked Bitch of the West'* back there, did ya?"

"Do you know...*I think I DID...*" said Jamie.

"Well, what's that thing you said is up in the penthouse?" Freddie asked.

"I don't think you are *ready for who came back with me..."* remarked Jamie with a smile.

"So you have spent the last week in 18..."

"1849, to be exact!" interrupted Jamie.

"Wow...right where you wanted to be..." said Freddie.

"Not quite – 50 years earlier and I might've met Matthew Murray!"

"There must have been a *reason* for you to be there at that time..."

"Indeed there was – although, I *gained* from being there, I do believe the trip was for *Alicia and John Winters...*"

"You mean *John Watson?*" corrected Freddie.

"That's the thing – his father *changed their name by 19th century depot...*"

"What's that?"

"He had Alicia change the *two name boards on the side of his boat to 'Albert Winters and DAUGHTER'...*"

"Whoaaa...wait a minute – that means *you have changed history! That means that Albert and Doris Watson are your DIRECT RELATIVES and the start of YOUR FATHER'S BUSINESS!*"

"I suppose we have...I hope you didn't show our Victoria friends anything about *our world...*" said Jamie, quickly changing the subject.

"Ahem...uhh...nooo – I kept them indoors – *most of the time...*" replied Freddie.

"*Most of the time?*" repeated Jamie, raising an eyebrow.

"Well, you know – I may have taken them to the odd *museum or two...*I only let them see things from their *own time.*"

"And how did they get to these *museums*, Freddie?"

"Well...um...yaknow...*taxis...that sort of thing...*"

"Taxis...and BUSES, Freddie?!!"

"And...maybe the *odd train to York...*"

"*Train to YORK!*"

"*Jamie – you are repeating my words.*"

"*I DON'T BELIEVE THIS! MY INSTRUCTIONS WERE SIMPLE! DON'T LET THEM SEE ANYTHING, AND INTERACT WITH THEM ONLY WHEN YOU HAVE TO!*"

A Switch in Time

"YES! Yes, I know – and believe me – I did *warn them about the space-time continuum and all of that*...but of course, they hadn't seen 'Back to the Future'. I also may have inadvertently..."

"YOU MIGHT'VE INADVERTANTLY WHAT, FREDDIE!"

"I...I may have...or rather, you could say, I sort of, like...fell in love with and married Alice..."

The car screeched to a halt.

"Fallen in love and married *Alice?*"

"You're doing that repeating my words again, Jamie..."

"Did you...*you know*...with her??"

"Well, umm..."

"Oh MY GOD! WHAT IF YOU'VE MADE HER PREGNANT!"

"Um...I don't think I did...because, there were *physical differences* between us that caused a slight problem."

"No! STOP THERE! I DON'T WANT THE SORDID DETAILS...BUT, FREDDIE, DAMN! WHAT WERE YA THINKING??"

"Well...that's *charming* coming from the man who *went back in time and changed something to make himself RICH.*"

"That is *not now it happened Freddie and you KNOW IT!* Let's stop this, and hope we both haven't caused too much damage to the space-time continuum."

"Okay, Doc – It's all gotten too *heavy*..." said Freddie with a smile.

The two friends pulled up outside what was going to be the BEST PRESERVED RAILWAY IN THE WORLD, and exited the car.

On entering the main building, they both quickly went downstairs to the cellar. The white brick was on the floor where Freddie left it the week before.

"Let's move those four bricks below the hole left by that brick that you took out." Said Jamie.

"Okay." Said Freddie, picking up the hammer and chisel, beginning to tap away at the bricks.

Sure enough, the tin box was *there*. Jamie quickly opened it, and the plans were still inside.

"Wow! These are plans for our *loco*!"

"I know." Said Jamie with a smug smile.

"How did you manage *this*?" asked Freddie.

"I got a job for John…an *apprenticeship…in this very factory…*"

"I thought this was a *station*." Remarked Freddie.

"So did I – but, originally, it was a *factory that made industrial locomotives…including OURS. Wait until you see what is behind that wall and under these stone floor slabs!"*

"What?" asked Freddie eagerly.

"All the casts that we need for replacement parts for our *engine*."

"Ohh…well done you!" said Freddie.

"Let's just see if these slabs will lift."

At that point, someone came in upstairs. Jamie climbed up the ladder, closely followed by Freddie.

"Hello Lee – what brings *you* here?" asked Jamie.

"Two Victorians, and a shaggy dog story about Mennonites…"

Turning to Freddie, Jamie asked, "Can you throw some light on this?"

"Well…I *may have let John Watson work with Lee for awhile…I thought it might keep his mind off of MODERN THINGS if I surrounded him with Victorian machinery."* Said an uneasy Freddie.

"Actually, that may help in his development of becoming an engineer..." said Jamie.

"Somebody explain this to me – or there is *no more using my workrooms and lathes*!" interrupted Lee.

"You may change your mind about that *when you see what I've discovered downstairs*..." said Freddie.

All three men trundled down the ladder.

"I was about to lift these stones to see what lies underneath them...the thing is...*I already know.*" Said Jamie.

"What? Let me guess – some old, used, worn-out moulds?" offered Lee sarcastically.

"On the contrary, my dear fellow, what we have here is *brand spanking new. Never used mouldings for the VERY ENGINE WE OWN...*"

Lee Coates looked on in disbelief as Freddie lifted the first stone with a crowbar, and the first moulding was uncovered.

"How could you have known that! There is moss all around it – that stone hasn't been moved *for years*!"

"Ohh, Lee...I know *much more than that...concealed within the wall behind me is a furnace, also never used...*"

"How can this be!" Lee asked, gobsmacked.

"Lee – I *need you to open your mind and LISTEN to what I have to say. I was standing in this VERY ROOM the day before yesterday...in the year 1849...*" said Jamie.

Jamie looked at Lee and saw the *turmoil and confusion* in his face. Turning to Freddie, he said, "Fancy a pint, you two? I will explain *everything...*"

"I don't mind if we do, *mystery boy*...we have a lot to discuss!" answered Freddie.

John Paul Bernett

The three friends walked to the Railway Public House, and the strangest afternoon conversation that had ever taken place between these three friends began.

Alicia took a look around the spacious penthouse that was *for her alone*. She knew there were people living in overcrowded houses…and even people living on the streets. Up until now, *she had never given them a second's thought.* Up until a week ago – she lived on *Planet Alicia*, and didn't GIVE A DAMN about anybody else but *herself*. She just stood, staring at her opulent surroundings, thinking of how *shallow her life really was.* She *now knew what life was – and she had experienced motherly love for the first time in her pathetic, useless existence.* She was too emotional to do anything today – she needed a *plan of action.* But what she needed *most of all* was for her head to clear for what she had to do. There was a lot to put right – but she had the time to do it. Her ponderings took up all of the afternoon and most of the evening, and now it was time for bed. One part of her sumptuous apartment that she still liked was the bedroom. Before bed she removed the slightly-uncomfortable 21st century clothes and took a bath.

Whilst bathing, she noticed the dark stain of *coal dust* under her nails. She remembered saying how Albert and Doris' daughter *smelled…and how bad her hygiene was.* This made her sad. It was yet another reminder of her old shallow self. However, that thought was replaced by the thought of someone who had never seen a proper bath…being able to *luxuriate in this one for a week…and that brought a smile back to her lips.*

As one hour slowly drifted into another, Alicia Winters' mind still could not allow her the sleep she so desperately wanted. She was going over in *fine detail* the events of the past week. The week that had started *so ordinarily* – ordinary by *her standards at least. This made her VERY SURE of what to do next.* Indeed – things were going to be different – for her, and for her *family*. Things would *never be the same again. As she finally drifted into*

A Switch in Time

slumber, her dreams took her to the people, and deeds, that she would PUT RIGHT, as she relived the past joyful seven days.

Today was Wednesday, it was 9 a.m., and the first act of the rest of this young girl's life was taking place. She was at the solicitor's office filling in the papers of dipole to officially change her name from *Alicia to Alice Winters*. She took the document from her solicitor and signed it again in her *new name* at another solicitor's office, and her first job was done.

Next, she made her way to Beacroft & Dunne – the estate agent from whom her father had purchased her the penthouse. As the old door clicked against the brass bell on the jorm, everyone inside felt a sense of *impending doom* as *'Cruella de Bitch'* walked in.

'Alice', as she was now called, was the *last person they expected to walk in*, and her eyes widened as she saw Ian Steele sitting at his desk, indeed not having been *replaced.*

"I can explain, Miss Winters…" said a red-faced Graham Dunne.

"I don't think there is any need for *explanations*, Mr. Dunne – it is *quite clear to me that you must have thought I was some kind of spoilt bitch, and you were not going to take any notice of what I had said!*"

"Umm…" Graham Dunne's necktie seemed to be *choking him* as he searched for the words to say to her…because all she had just said was *true.*

"Well – I *intend to deal with this forthwith, and APOLOGIZE for my behaviour, Mr. Dunne. You were right – I WAS a spoilt bitch. I most certainly should NOT have done what I did.* Mr. Steele…*you are the one I need to apologize to the MOST.* Your patience is *exemplary.* How you kept your cool while I was being *so rude to you* is UNBELIEVABLE. If the roles had been reversed, I would have *slapped you SO HARD.* So to you, I *humbly apologize, and would like you to accept this gift from me as a token of my appreciation for your EXCELLENT WORK.*"

Alice handed over an envelope to Ian Steele, saying, "Please open it when I leave. I do not want...nor do I *deserve*...a thank you. I just *hope* it goes some way towards patching things up between us. Mr. Beacroft, I am in need of an *old factory building I can have redeveloped* – it is to be rebuilt as a Youth Hostel, where young people who are living on the streets can stay. Could I please leave that in your very capable hands? The larger the building, the better; expense is *no object.*"

With that, she bid everyone a good day and left the building.

Everybody in that office, from William Henry Beacroft right down to the young lad who ran errands was amazed and agog as they all stared at the door swinging shut behind Miss Alice Winters. Then, all eyes turned towards Ian Steele, who, still in disbelief, began to cut the top of the envelope with his letter opener.

"It's a *car log book and a set of keys...for a MERCEDES BENZ SLS CLASS!*"

"What! The convertible?" asked Graham Dunne.

"Yes! *And it isn't even a year old...*" said Ian Steele.

"She might be a cow – but when she apologizes she does it in style!" observed Graham.

"Well I would say *apology accepted*!" said the young man as he ran out of the office to the awaiting 2013 Mercedes Benz SLS Class parked outside.

As he looked around, he could not see Alice in order to thank her, so he depressed the button on the fob and opened the door to his new car...and a *more stable future...*

Alice was feeling a tad hungry, because she had been in such a hurry that morning she had forgotten breakfast. She called into a café opposite the market on Vicar Lane. Once inside, she sat down, and for the first time, perused an *ordinary café menu*. The bald-headed man behind the counter said, "Hello, there! It's nice to see you again!"

A Switch in Time

Alice looked confused and said, "You must be mistaken, sir – I've never been in here before."

"But only last week…you were here with a tall gentleman and a young lad around 16…"

"Not me, I'm afraid!" she said with a smile.

"WOW. Well all I can say is, *you have a double miss.* Now, what can I get you?"

"What would you recommend?"

"Now that would depend on *how hungry you are miss…I can do everything from a belly-buster breakfast with two eggs, four rashers of bacon, four sausages, black pudding, tomatoes, beans, fry bread, toast and tea…*"

Alice gulped.

"…right down to a bacon butty."

"I think I will have a bacon butty, please…oh, and a cup of tea."

"Bacon butty and tea coming up!" said the cheery café owner.

Alice sat back in her rather uncomfortable chair and wondered who this woman was that had looked like her. Then she thought…*a woman who looked just like her, and a younger teenager…could that have been Alice and John??*

Her thoughts were broken by the arrival of the hot bacon sandwich. It smelled *divine*…and Alice, just like her Victorian namesake, was about to indulge in a type of food she had *never experienced before – a greasy bacon butty.*

As she bit into that culinary delight, it sent her rather-educated and posh taste buds into *gastronomic meltdown.* The café owner saw her expression and said, "You're eating that like you have never eaten one before!"

With part of her sandwich still in her mouth, she said, "It's *wonderful!*" then thought of what her instructor in etiquette would think of her at her finishing school in Switzerland, and a little chuckle came.

After her breakfast, for reasons unbeknownst to her, she made her way to her father's main storage depot. This was a place she had *never* visited before. But she felt she *had to go there* before she met up with her parents. As she walked through the gates and into the main area of the depot, a large articulated wagon pulled into the yard. The massive truck came to a halt with the sound of its air brakes de-pressurizing. The driver's door swung open, and to Alice's *amazement – her MOTHER jumped from the cab to the ground, her face stained with OIL and GRIME.* As she landed, she looked at Alice and said, "Where were YOU this morning when I need ya?"

Alice stared at the person standing in front of her, and in a disbelieving voice said, *"Mother…is that…you?"*

"Of COURSE it's me you SILLY GIRL! You weren't around this morning when the driver rang in sick, and I wasn't about to let your *poor father* do it again! He works too hard as it is! But now you are here, can you take it to Warehouse 32 for me and have Jim unload it?"

"Ok." Said Alice as she climbed the ladder into the cab and pulled away towards the warehouses. She began to chuckle and said out loud to herself, *"What am I doing…I can't drive a truck!"* as she put the juggernaut into 2nd gear and drove *straight to Warehouse no. 32.* *"And how did I know where this warehouse is?"* she said with a giggle.

After reversing it into the loading bay, she shouted, "Jim – Bay 12 ready to unload!"

A voice from behind shouted back, "I'm on it Alice!"

A Switch in Time

This made Alice stop in her tracks. What was going ON?? Her mother was *dirty and had just brought in a delivery…both she and her mother could DRIVE A TRUCK…but strangest of ALL…this guy Jim KNEW HER NAME WAS ALICE…*

She made her way to the office. All the workers she passed said, "Good morning, Alice!" and she replied to each one *by name. How could this be??*

Once inside the main office, the secretary said, "Good morning, Alice, your father is expecting you."

"Thank you, Janet." Said Alice, again looking puzzled.

Once in her father's office she made her way to his desk.

"Princess, you are *here!"* He stood up and gave her a kiss on her cheek.

"Hahaaa! So much for telling her off!" chided her mother with a smile.

"You are *late back from your holidays…but now that you are back, EVERYTHING IS OK."*

"Well, are *you* going to tell her, or shall I?" said Alice's mother.

"We have decided that I should *'hang my boots' – it's time for me to retire. So, you are now going to be NUMBER ONE AROUND HERE! You have proven yourself AGAIN AND AGAIN that you can do the job…so, if you want the position, it's YOURS!"*

"Well, this isn't going as I had thought…but, HELL YEAH! ANOTHER BLOW FOR THE SUFFRAGETTES!" said Alice.

"*Suffragettes?"* repeated her father.

"It doesn't matter. So – what will you two *do* in your retirement?" she asked.

"Well, obviously your mother will be spending even *more time* helping Jamie with his train set…"

"*Preserved RAILWAY…"* Interrupted his wife.

"Yaknow what them two are like – thick as *thieves, always have been...*"

Alice bit her lip in *disbelief,* trying to hold back laughter at what she had just heard.

"And I will finally get to write about the firm's *history – right back to old Albert – to whom we all owe a GREAT DEAL OF GRATITUDE."*

"Some of us *more than you will EVER KNOW, dad...I might be able to help you with that..."* offered Alice, with a wry smile. "But for now, I have *one or two things to do, so I shall ask the BOSS if it's ok for me to go...*wait a minute...I *am the boss! YES, I CAN GO! THANK ME VERY MUCH! I'LL CATCH YA'LL LATER, AT HOME!"*

With that, Alice took a taxi to her brother's railway.

As soon as she arrived, she ran towards the now near-finished station. A little further down the line was the old building, where she found Jamie.

"Jamie...you won't believe it...our mother is *normal! She can drive a truck! I can drive a truck! Our dad..."*

"Alice! Alice, calm down!" interrupted Jamie.

"And that's *another thing...everybody knows that my name is Alice now – and I only changed it THIS MORNING!"*

"You're not the only one sis – look around you. This place was like it was when I left it a week ago…but as soon as Freddie and I took the plans that I had hidden in the wall...while we were at the pub, things began to *alter! When I got back from the pub, I found it like this!"*

Jamie showed Alice around the almost-rebuilt railway. He took her down into the cellar and showed her where he had removed the white brick.

A Switch in Time

"This is how I got the plans for the engine...and the *notes on where everything was, back into THIS CENTURY.* But most of all, this note is how I told Freddie to go to your penthouse and look after John and Alice! After chatting with Freddie at the pub, I got the impression that John would have stepped STRAIGHT INTO MY SHOES AT THE FACTORY. Also I think Freddie was quite sweet on Alice..."

"Ohh...Freddie...I had better go and try to make my peace with him. Where is he?"

"I don't really know...he had some bad news today, and eventually he just wanted to *be alone."*

"Okay then, I will see you later...I need to *think about all of this."*

"Okay sis..." said Jamie. The two siblings embraced each other.

Alice walked away trying to work out what had happened. Had she and her brother caused an alternative future for themselves? Had they *really been time travelling?* Then came the thought of what good she could start doing with her *endless millions...*that brought a smile to her face. She looked up and saw the Leeds Minster clock tower. She walked through the gates and into the church yard and began to peruse the graves, remembering her *awful comment* just a week ago. She came across a young man, kneeling at a grave. She felt *sad* for him and looked at the gravestone. A *shiver went down her spine as she read:*

Albert Winters – Beloved Husband & Father 1800 - 1868

Doris Winters – Wife of the Above 1800 - 1870

John Winters – Son 1832 - 1891

Alice Chambers-Winter – Daughter 1821 - 1901

Freddie Chambers heard Alice as she caught her breath, and turned around.

"Alice…is that…you?"

Upon hearing the once-loathed friend of her brother's voice, something *primeval stirred in her psyche. Blood started rushing through her veins…a myriad of memories came flooding back, as if to chase the monster away that used to dwell within her. In that one definitive MOMENT IN TIME, Alicia was cast into the four winds, and Alice LIVED AGAIN, as surely as if she had risen from the grave itself.* She felt REBORN, and was as giddy as a school child…and all of her thoughts had been OVERTAKEN by the most POWERFUL FEELING OF LOVE SHE HAD EVER EXPERIENCED.

She took a deep breath, and exclaimed, "Yes, my Freddie…I am here."

Freddie jumped up from his squatting position, and tears of sadness were replaced with *tears of joy.* He took hold of Alice and lifted her from the ground, covering her face in kisses. Alice flung her arms around him and said, "I am *here, my love…*", and kissed him passionately.

"We will be together FOREVER…" said Freddie.

Their embrace seemed to go on forever. They were *young lovers at the dawn of their new life together. As they walked away from the grave, arm-in-arm, three ghostly figures – Albert, Doris, and their son John, were left behind, looking on…all of them happy about the outcome of a SWITCH IN TIME.*

Time waits for no-one…and until 'death do we part' – not so! If your love is strong enough you WILL MEET AGAIN…and find that time THEN is as time NOW…IS AS TIME WILL BE.

THE END

Be Happy

John Paul Bernett

JP Bernett

I would like to thank my wife Beverly Gail Bernett for all her hard work during the writing of this book

I would also like to thank Gavin Johnson and Lee Coats of

V-Edition Media for their excellent cover design

Website - htttps://www.facebook.com/JpBernettAuthornb

A Switch in Time

John Paul Bernett